Filthy

A Breakthrough Book no. 46

Filthy the Man

Stories by Gerald Flaherty

University of Missouri Press
Columbia, 1985

Library of Congress Cataloging in Publication Data

Flaherty, Gerald.
    Filthy the man.

    (A Breakthrough book ; no. 46)
    I. Title. II. Series.
PS3556.L275F5   1985   813'.54   84–21893
ISBN 0-8262-0463-5

"Something to Talk Like a Family About" was first published in *the new renaissance*, Spring 1980; "The Man Who Saved Himself" in *Negative Capability*, Winter 1984; and "Blood" in *Shankpainter*, Winter 1984.

The poems "I Sat Me Down," on p. 70, and "Summer," on p. 76, appear with the kind permission of their respective authors, Nicholas C. Fryar and Maya G. Flaherty.

Lines from the song "Photographs and Memories" by Jim Croce are used by permission of Blendingwell Music, Inc. Lines from the song "Don't You Make Me High (Don't You Feel My Leg)" by Danny Barker are used by permission of Popular Music Co.

The author is grateful to Stanford University for the opportunity to study with John L'Heureux as a Wallace Stegner Fellow, to the Fine Arts Work Center in Provincetown for his fellowship year there, to his family for its long support, and especially to his friend, Arthur Edelstein, for his encouragement and direction.

Production of this book was funded in part by a grant from the National Endowment for the Arts.

for Maya and Colin

Contents

FILTHY THE MAN

Time flies. I'm past thirty. I was a kid at the time I'm talking about, and though none of the others involved were much older, most of them are dead. Jamie when his motorcycle hit a taxi in Saigon; Dekker laid up with pneumonia over the past summer, but nobody checked his liver and he died of cirrhosis; Brendan Corey murdered, or it was an accident I'd like to think, by Hump Munga, who's still running; Murray, he OD'd in his sister's bathroom; and don't let me forget Phil, who got to be a pimp and was disemboweled by one of his business rivals in a South End hallway. Time flies, all right, and let us all be grateful.

We were standing on the corner one night, entertained by this elderly guy. God only knows why we stayed there, kicking our toes against the curb to fight the cold, fanning steam and eating popcorn, huddling smokes in a doorway. Call it fellowship, or say nobody went home at nine on a Friday night. The guy did "an old softshoe," my folks used to call it.

"I'll tell you how my head shrunk," he said.

To prolong the show, Murray asked how. A big kid, fat more than anything, Murray didn't give a hoot who he needled.

"I was sitting there, about where you're sitting right now," he said (Murray, like the rest of us, was standing), "and all of a sudden for some reason I felt my forehead."

"Burning with fever," Murray said.

"No, no. I had my hand up to my head, here, and I could span it, no kidding."

"Like a wrench. Wasn't screwed on right."

"I've got a small hand. So help me, but it felt like if I put the heel of my palm on the one temple the tips of my fingers could stretch all the way around to the other side. My head had gotten much smaller."

"A real pinhead, what you call it," Murray said to him. "Pinhead."

"Now you're just out to make fun of it, but it happened," he said, before falling back into the mumbo jumbo a lot of those raggy old duffers can talk to each other.

The few girls with us had all run for a Mercury early on, convincing each other the driver at least looked familiar, although he never did come to a full stop. We'd take the next ride ourselves, we were all thinking. Get off the Ave. Just then Filthy Phil rolled up in an old, spot-primed DeSoto, the window on the driver's side all taped in splinters where he'd popped it with his fist. Always punching this or that, full of himself.

He was by himself. Short brown leather jacket unzipped and cracked like a house peeling. Over a T-shirt in that cold. Shock of off-blond hair held down with petroleum jelly. The T-shirt that color you get by leaving something white for months in a hamper. At twenty-five or so he was a man who'd outlived his timeliness. Phil was older than the rest of us, whose ages ranged from my own barely seventeen to Dekker's twenty. He was still single, and his few older friends never said he had parents. The name "Filthy Phil," a play on his last name, Phillips, had stuck with him from as far back as I can remember, when he was always under someone's car in the street—though he was Phil to his face.

Once out on the sidewalk he stretched his chest impressively, going up on his toes briefly to medium height before demanding a beer from Jamie.

"No got," Jamie said, the voice only just making it out of his small body. He looked pointedly around at me, his one true friend (the look said), and likely second. Phil had begun to toe a pit in the curb as if he might fly at him out of a sprinter's block. Phil only hit car windows and hollow doors, according to my information, but I was just as glad he hadn't taken the dislike to me that he had to Jamie.

We were doomed to a good time. Dekker wheeled in and parked over the crosswalk. With plenty of other parking space it was a sort of defiance, and he'd regularly use that spot like a starting line to spin rubber. Up front he had Stevie Cole, a tough little rat, and Hump Munga was alone in the back seat. Join us, they said. Phil volunteered his car for the overflow. Jamie jumped into the back with Munga and shot me a look to get in quick. He reached over me for the door handle, leaving Murray to ride alone with Phil.

We were a procession in no time. Stevie began rummaging in the glove compartment. For a piece of cloth, he said. Not finding it there he had me search in back under everyone's feet. When I couldn't find one he scowled and whipped out his handkerchief.

"Gimme another snot rag," he ordered.

Dekker looked away through the windshield. What fool would give over his hanky in that weather?

"Don't keep one on me," I said.

Jamie lied too, wiping his nose with his index finger so Stevie would believe him. And Munga, his face, the lovely absence there. There was a straight answer. But by then Stevie had pulled off his coat, a beige three-quarter length with the collar up. He had a black shirt under it and he took that off.

"Hey *man*," Dekker was telling him now from behind the wheel.

This was a puzzle all right, Jamie and I might have been saying with the looks we gave each other. Stevie was bare from the waist up. Munga never changed his expression, which is to say he remained expressionless. I still insist Munga was bright enough, maybe more than that, he'd just never made it in high school. Untapped, more or less, he read on his own they tell me. A natural build. Almost benign, you'd think, except for that. Have you got all this? We're missing two yet, plus Phil's "auntie," as he called her.

But wait. Stevie folded his shirt neatly on the seat between himself and Dekker. He'd thrown his coat back on, elevating the collar so that was all you saw from the line of his shoulders. We cruised the city then for a solid hour, nursing bottles of beer in Dekker's new Pontiac with its heater amuck. All that time and their only words passed in a sense hand to hand, like a last beer. Jamie and I took to whispering uneasily to each other between cigarettes.

Finally the two in the front found what they wanted, and it was all too clear to me then what that was.

We parked out of the light. There was enough room behind for a trailer, but Phil wouldn't have been himself if he hadn't inched close enough to deface the bumper sticker over Dekker's exhaust: *Vote* McGILLICUDDY, *A Saint*, or something. Stevie was into the glove compartment again, this time taking a six-inch length of pipe and shoving it in his coat pocket. He jumped out with the shirt and hanky in his fist and went to work on the front license plate. Then around to the rear, minus the shirt, frantically motioning to Phil to back off so he could cover that one too.

"Screw! See ya later!" Stevie was shouting at him through his teeth.

"The liquor store?" I asked stupidly. "You're gonna rob it?"

"Not me," Dekker said. "Stevie's *doing* it. I'm doing him a favor. That's cool. What am I supposed to say, 'Don't do it'?"

I could see now why he hadn't just let Stevie take the plates off. That might be seen as complicity. I was losing all muscle control. Jamie had disappeared into his brother's air force parka. Thank Christ—who I'd heard moved in mysterious ways—for Hump Munga. Stevie was halfway across the street.

"Drive off," Hump said to Dekker.

Dekker, guardedly, said, "Wanna? You know how *pissed* he'll be?"

Jamie reappeared out of the parka as we got in gear and Munga signaled out the window for Phil to follow. Stevie, seeing both cars bolt, started chasing after us down the white line. Phil stopped and let him in finally and we headed home to the corner, Jamie and I, out of relief, laughing so bad we couldn't have popped our own bottle caps. Even with a church key. Stevie had evidently taken that with him, too. His spare "piece." Jamie rolled over into the front seat and somehow got everyone's open under the dash. I could see he was happy, riding shotgun, in charge of the last few beers for some real hard guys.

We got back to the corner in a freezing drizzle. Phil, trailing Murray and Stevie, piled in the Pontiac with us for a conference. Brendan Corey and Walter Donnelly came out of the drugstore and stood by on the curb. There was another guy there named Eddie Galvin and Dekker made us lock all the doors on him. Eddie could have been thirty, and he'd talk your ear off. Always with some strange headgear, extremes you might say, yarmulkes, or a raccoon cap that night, the end result of a motorcycle accident when he was bareheaded, my mother told me.

I should tell you Stevie wasn't that mad. All he said to Dekker was that there'd been some scruffy old couple in the liquor store with a bag full of empties, wanting their deposits back. "Looked like your mom and dad," he said. "Bad timing."

But the question was where to go. Everyone else lived at home with their folks, so Phil volunteered his place, seeming happy to do that for eight of his friends. He was renting a single room from his aunt in a brick tenement a few blocks away. So Phil and Murray got out and took Corey and Walter Donnelly in the other car. Eddie we ditched. In an odd way it was a good thing there were no girls, I thought, partly out of respect, but also because of their cheery habit of breaking into song in a crowded automobile. We pooled a lot of change and small bills on the way and had Phil, the only one old enough, pick up three cases of Rheingold, more popcorn, and a carton of Luckys.

Downstairs in his hallway Phil cautioned us about talking or dropping our shoes as we snaked in in our socks. His aunt managed the building and had a small apartment on the third floor, down the hall from his room. He was just another boarder, he told us, but she'd sometimes carry him for a week or two, so everyone had to get serious, leapfrogging like commandos with the beer.

The real obstacles were all in his room. A cardboard wardrobe, an unmade double bed, nightstand, a long, mirrored dresser. The wardrobe was imitation mahogany laid in a pattern like zebra stripes, and all the wood stuff was in the dark lacquer finish I've come to associate with my grandfather's sickroom.

There was an overstuffed armchair, apparently used as a hamper. There was an old, single-unit hi-fi on the nightstand and a gold wastebucket by the wardrobe. Two windows with green pull shades faced out on the Avenue through a curved wall. Over there he had three vending machines. They were metallic gray, the sort with the tall mirror up over the knobs, and normally sold things like Chicklets and Lifesavers, or combs and toilet accessories. He wouldn't say how he got them, but he made it clear to Stevie that he already had a partner. I thought we could all be thankful for the overhead light.

Somehow we settled in. Phil casually shucked his jacket so everyone could admire his build through the yellowed T-shirt. The rest of us piled our coats neatly over his in the middle of the bed, and Jamie politely asked Stevie for the church key back. Then there was a lot of grabbing for the beer, and Jamie only got to open two of them. As if to rub it in, Phil opened his with his teeth.

Walter Donnelly and I sat on opposite arms of the only chair, talking and eating popcorn over the mounds of Phil's dirty laundry. Walter's father had died around the time. Hump Munga mentioned a warm meeting with Mr. Donnelly once in a bar where they both could get served.

"Sure," Walter said, "my old man's had a drink in every armpit gin mill in the city. Just let me tell you he was always wearing a cashmere topcoat and a good-looking pair of shoes."

"That your mother must have paid for," Murray added, but Walter, with his strangely animated look, like a ventriloquist's dummy, had already let us know that it was okay to laugh.

Walter was a case. He and Corey and Jamie and I were graduating from high school in the spring. As a sophomore Walter had changed his birth certificate to eighteen so he could be a part-time attendant in the mental hospital where they kept his brother Leo, who caught something as a kid, I don't know. Knock on wood. Which leaves us Corey, a tall, good-looking guy you'd have expected to get a scholarship. Never did. Moody kind of guy. Talked politics. He'd run for something later, I predicted. After college, he thought. Good luck was my reaction, but enough of that.

Phil wouldn't let anybody play with the knobs on his vending machines, so Dekker and Stevie took on Munga and Corey at whist for nickels. Walter took over the hi-fi, sitting with the others on what was once a wall-to-wall carpet, although there wasn't what you'd call a record collection. Fats Domino. Singing chipmunks. But Walter was easily entertained.

Not Phil's auntie. She was at the door in a flash, up in arms.

"Who's *in* there?" she wanted to know.

"No one," Phil told her.

"Then open the door!"

"A few of my friends, auntie." Someone had to interpret his crude hand signals for Walter, who reluctantly shut the record off.

"What friends?" she said.

"New guys," he told her obscurely. "Be gone shortly."

"Better be," she said.

Meanwhile, Walter had put the back of his head up to the hi-fi and was telling Corey how he could hear his own heart beating between his ears.

"Sounds a little like the creak in an old rocking chair," Walter said. "Twisting leather! Under my skin, a belt tightening over my bones."

Corey bobbed his head knowledgeably.

"Birds chirping," Murray said under his breath.

Walter caught that. "Am I listening to a man who buys pants with his suits?" he asked.

"At least try to make believe you're all there," Murray told him, daffily outgunned.

We could hear the aunt shuffle off grumping, mad as a wet hen. Phil too, mortified, a blowfish with his chest. He was on Jamie's case like poor auntie on the door.

"Twerp!" he snapped. Somehow to Jamie that just meant Phil wanted another beer. He quickly handed one to me to hand Phil, which put me directly in the man's path, caught in the narrow passage between the end of the bed and the dresser. Phil glared over my shoulder at Jamie, then snatched the beer from my hand.

The next minute he wanted to arm wrestle. He'd broken his

elbow once, he sneered at Jamie, and now it was impossible for any mortal to flatten the arm. Jamie took me aside. (What with the four playing cards on the floor on the far side of the bed, Murray up against a vending machine kibitzing, and Walter underfoot at the hi-fi, that was not the rush hour dilemma it sounds like.) Jamie and I grouped by the armchair, with Phil stewing across the room against the wardrobe. He came directly to the point: Would I save his life, as Phil was going to keep him in the room when everyone left and murder him?

"Nothing less?"

"No joke," he said. "He told me on the way up. He hates me I don't know why. Cause I'm small?"

So in that case what had he come up for?

"I was with you!" he reminded me.

The match was made. As Jamie's stand-in I would arm wrestle Phil on the dresser, thereby advertising my support of my friend, who had taken the bull by the horns as it were, and handed me the cape.

Even Corey showed some interest, or maybe he was just anxious to keep his mind off his bladder. Sure enough the only john was down the hall, by auntie's inner sanctum. ("No chance," Phil had already told us in that regard.) We gathered around the dresser. My opponent was curiously aglow. I was a few inches taller but he was much bigger, if you see what I mean. In fairness I did enjoy a growing sense of necessity via the look on Jamie's face, plus an unexpected boost from Hump Munga, the one truly *bad* actor in the lot. "Filthy's a bum," he whispered to me. We lock thumbs and Murray yelled go.

Breathing athletically, we hunkered down like that for close to a minute, Filthy Phil, a grown man, and me, relatively untouched by time and alcohol. If I lost I thought I could count on my three schoolmates for some sort of protection. And if I won, well. It was all in the wrist anyway, I remembered an older cousin once advising me. No one had told Phil that, because I had his hand bent in short order at a right angle to his forearm. He was still bold enough to call that a strategy, claim he was relying on the jerry-built elbow all the time, but he'd slurred his words and the pressure was on. Soon he was breaking wind. So much for the elbow. Then it was over.

Now, for me, here was the very first time I'd beaten an adult at anything. For Phil, suddenly he wanted to talk vending machines with that other little ballbuster, Stevie. Jamie looked like he might lead a cheer. The others, well, it was Phil's place, they had to make out like nothing had happened.

But I had ascended to something. Everyone had to piss and Jamie was the first to look to me. I looked sideways at Phil, and his sour expression was straight-up. Good luck to you, bud, it said. Luck? I'd won my moment with a perfect act of strength and he knew it. Luck. That's for the rest of your life.

"Use the bottles," I said. They gathered up the empties. Corey looked like he may have been in pain with cramps, but he left the first attempt to Jamie (who by association had become something of a leader here). After that when we took our bottles we stood over the wastebucket. It was metal, which would do, oval-rimmed, about a foot high, and out of decorum I pushed it deep into the corner next to Phil's cardboard wardrobe. They were to place their refilled bottles on top of this closet, I instructed them, and maintain a bank of empties on the dresser. Phil acknowledged the logic. He took two. Now I was studying alternatives.

Nevertheless things went smoothly for an hour or more. Auntie came back once and banged like the hammers of hell.

"They're going, auntie," Phil promised.

"My other boarders!" she hollered through the door.

Corey said he was leaving anyway. "They're all leaving, auntie," Phil shouted back.

"Send them out," she said.

"They're not ready," he said.

She had the last word. "Make it snappy!" or the like. We caught her drift.

"I'm leaving anyway," Corey said.

"In that case," Phil told him, "pretend you're as many guys as you can. Stamp on the stairs, slam the door downstairs, see, say good-bye a lot."

Phil shoved him out into the hall before anyone could say good-bye, but Corey was a stand-up guy.

"See ya!" rang back at us in his own voice, and blocking his nose, "So longa!" then "Take care now!" from way back in his throat.

We heard him stamping on the worn treads and the next thing, bang! Phil tiptoed out into the hall. We could hear auntie running. Phil scurried back in and bolted the door.

"Is he awright?" Walter said.

Phil threw up his hands. "He's just laying there, that shithead."

I offered to go and check on him, but auntie was at the door. Stevie said to screw her; he was jousting with one of Phil's vending machines in order to catch a glimpse of Corey, who'd been spotted by Munga out a front window, staggering across the streetcar tracks. Phil was still insisting everyone had left.

"I'll be the judge of that!" she said. Then the clincher: "You want a room to live in, or out in the street?"

"I'm almost in bed, auntie," he said. "Hold it."

He mimed an air attack, indicating we should all hit the deck, and then tore his pants off. The coats he heaved over the side of the bed onto Dekker. One of us jumped behind a vending machine, someone else upset the bucket getting in the corner beside the wardrobe. The rest, bar me, were sitting cross-legged on the floor behind one corner of the bed. All smoking. In those days six beers could get to me good. And I was intrigued, watching this. Filthy killed the lights. By then he'd also unbolted the door, and was modestly trying to shield himself with it. I began to lower myself by stages into a tight corner between the armchair and one end of the dresser. Someone shoved my foot out with enough force to knock me over onto the chair, where I had to cover myself with T-shirts, socks, old sheets, Phil's wash. That or be seen. He didn't own a real laundry bag I suppose. I cleared an air hole for my cigarette.

It was so dark that all I could see out of that heap were the smoldering heads of seven other cigarettes. Even Phil had kept his. Everywhere I turned, these and the red ON light on the hi-fi. From the position of one glowing butt I could imagine the back of Walter's head up against the speaker. What could she have thought? Every drag a sudden flare, I'm surprised no one lit a match.

What I saw then always seemed so funny I could just never tell anyone. Plopped in that shitty armchair, I knew I'd outlive them all. Saw it, period. And not because I was still high from whipping Phil, or from the beer either. I felt strong, sure, but superior no. What it made me feel like, to tell the truth, is that I'd be missing something, something, for the rest of my life. Something they all seemed to know, whether they knew it or not. Left out, I guess I felt, but normal. But let's not talk normalcy now. Phil's voice is still clear as a bell.

"See auntie," he said, "all gone."

She leaned in from the hall through the narrow opening he'd allowed her. "Good!" she said. "But clean it up."

I'll never know how we didn't all laugh.

The rest I'll cut short. We ran out of empties. We pissed in the wastebucket. That leaked. We pissed out the window at daybreak. Nothing lewd, understand, we were in a bind. Stick any eight guys in a room like that. After that, though, we left. Sunny morning, biting cold. Kind of morning you had to take your bike in a taxi, as Walter put it, but no one had a bicycle.

What can I add? It broke up. Phil didn't want us to go. Then he tried to get me to get the others to take all the bottles out. Good luck. Jamie and I decided right there to quit school and join the army, go where it was warm. We'd go home first, get some sleep, and one of us was supposed to call for the other and haul our butts in to a recruiting station. I might have gotten up for supper, as I recall. Him, too. After graduation I got my parents' written consent and enlisted by myself. Jamie had lost the calling by then. Did my time, for what it was worth. He did, later, get drafted, and you know the rest. Stevie's in the can. Murray's gone. I've met Walter when he's recognized me, and met him when he hasn't. Something snapped there. Corey and I didn't bump into each other to speak of for several years after I got out of the service, when he was what you'd call "on his way." The story about Munga goes that to this day he's doing a penance for stabbing him, scouring the world for the one answer to everything. Dekker, I said already. Phil I've also told you.

I'm comfortably out of the city now. Lawn, garden, wonderful wife, kids, foreman's rates, bet on it. Doesn't affect me, like you'd hear them say passing up a joint years ago.

Oh, there are a few things I miss. You know a city, shimmering neon on the wet asphalt, rain washing the smell of piss and popcorn out of dark corners of the old neighborhoods. Little excitements, the characters. Filthy and so many other of them. I've milked it all for stories. History to the offspring. And my apologies to Filthy the man, but me here to tell it.

THE MAIN CHANCE

Brian Shea did the last two years of his army hitch in the Aleutian Islands. Most of the men had spent their off-duty hours indoors, gambling. Brian had started running, seen a lot of movies, and saved his money. It could have been Vietnam, his mother reminded him in each of her letters.

After processing out at Oakland, he stayed two weeks with ex-army buddies in San Francisco, where he spent a thousand dollars having fun. But when the homesickness of the previous two years suddenly returned, he'd booked the next nonstop flight to Boston.

On this, his first morning home, his mother and two younger sisters were already off at work and his father was cooking hotcakes for Uncle Buster, who sat at the kitchen table calling out the Help Wanted ads like a bingo announcer.

"Security guard! Parking lot attendant! Models and dancers they want!"

Brian lay under a thin blanket on the living room couch. With twenty-four hundred dollars in traveler's checks there beside his wallet on the mantel, he had no intention of getting up yet. Not for a meal or a job. He was home, on his own time now.

"Wish I had a chauffeur's license for this one," he heard his uncle say. "Lookit here, drive some old bat around shopping in a big '75 Mercedes! You above housepainting, Brian?"

"I'm all set," Brian called back over the rumble of a truck that seemed to shake every board in the old three-family house. Their house. His, one day, he hoped.

"You take that one," he said.

"How set?" his uncle asked in a more respectful voice.

Buster was the best. He was younger than Brian's father, but had retired early as a warehouseman after hurting his back. As far as Brian knew he'd always lived with them. He had his small pension and reduced social security. Mondays, like clockwork, he rode the Blue Line out to Wonderland to bet on the dogs, sometimes taking one of the older women he met at church bingos. And Brian was his favorite in the family.

"All set, thanks," Brian said.

Fully awake, he began to feel hot and uncomfortable in the summer sunlight blazing through the venetian blinds. Some-one—out of habit, he supposed—had opened them while he slept.

He heard his father laughing. Would "Mr. Shea" be joining them for "brunch," he wanted to know.

"Sure," said Brian.

"Good," his father said shortly. "Ten bucks."

"All I got's traveler's checks."

"We take 'em," Buster hollered.

At least the old man hadn't lost his sense of humor. But then Brian thought that would be the last thing to go. Why had his mother never mentioned the long layoff in any of her letters? A touchy subject, apparently. More was left unsaid. Rooms had been put up as if for bid. Uncle Buster got Grandfather Hines's, which since the funeral—she did write to him about that—had only collected unused furniture; Brian's sister Emily, in with his sister Rita, got Uncle Buster's; and his father, who'd explained last night that he hadn't been sleeping well but how that was no reason Brian's mother should be deprived of a good night's rest, had taken a room of his own.

So, he had the couch for a while. No sweat. Rita or Emily, one of them would want a place of her own soon enough. Brian stood and admired the lean but solid look of his hairy chest in the mirror over the mantel. It was no big sweat about his father, either. He'd been installing carpets forever and they'd have to take him back soon. So. He fingered the deep impression of a baseball cleat that ran across the bridge of his nose. "Character," she'd said, just come right up to the bar in her G-string and said it.

"You know Belmondo?" she'd asked. "Jean-Paul, French actor, he had that beautiful broken nose?"

He'd pointed excitedly at his nose. "My uncle," he'd said.

Whether she believed that or not, he'd spent his last three days in San Francisco at her place, not far from where she worked in North Beach, and only had to pay for the first night. Three days that temporarily made up for a tour in the Aleutians. He looked down at the balled up blanket on the couch and tried to remember more of her, but all he could evoke was that flimsy costume. He turned back to the mirror. His father and his uncle were both stronger-looking men, true, but he'd stretched out in the army and now he was taller than either of them. In his gray athletic jersey and faded Wranglers he padded barefoot over the hallway linoleum to the kitchen.

"The dead awoke," said his father, "and appeared to many."

"He looks just fine," Buster said. "You look fine this morning."

"Just this morning?" Brian asked. He turned to his father. "So where are these hotcakes worth a sawbuck?"

"What lip!" Buster looked like he might offer a toast. Last night he'd talked about a short trip for just the two of them down to Atlantic City. "Buster thinks Rita and Emily will simply move away one day to a nicer place and forget about him, as if that's what girls are supposed to do," his mother had written in one of her letters. Now he was into the ads for some soft side work. He was the best.

Everything felt so easy again. Just being there in the big kitchen, the old-fashioned sink stuck up against the wall like a table on four white legs, the sound of the news on the Fitzgerald's radio across the alleyway. The banter, too. This wasn't army jive, all the forced good humor, the empty badmouthing of those endless card games. Army buddies. Saying it to himself made it sound like another language, when now everything felt so damn easy again.

His father served them hotcakes so big he'd had to make them one at a time in an oversized fry pan. After several minutes of concentrated eating, Buster looked up from the paper.

"There's no good reason a young guy can't work a while for minimum wages if there's nothing else," he told them. "That and the government'll pay for your college. Am I right, Will?"

"God takes care of those who take care of the woman who takes care of them," Brian's father answered.

"And that's some woman," Buster said.

"Once engaged to the nephew of the president of Ecuador," his father said, adding in a lower voice that she still had all the man's letters at the bottom of her hope chest.

"Well, even if she did take her eye off the main chance, she still got the right man," Buster said.

"Hell of a dancer, too. Studied ballet as a kid," his father said. He looked Brian up and down. "Danced once in a musical at the Shubert Theater."

"Good hotcakes," Brian said, unsure how else to join such a discussion of his mother. Although he was interested in the business about the Ecuadorian. Grandfather Hines had never let any of them forget it. What his daughter could have been. A queen, he made it sound like. Who took it seriously? He looked up from the sticky pool of syrup on his plate and his eyes met his father's.

"The bee's knees," said Buster.

That seemed to end it, with Brian wondering if Buster meant the hotcakes or his mother. He listened to the trickle of the re-frigerator straining to defrost, and the light clack of his father's upper and lower plates as they cut through his breakfast. From the alley below, there was the faint odor of garbage barrels standing without their lids in the compressed heat of an urban summer. He ate up.

"*Yes, we have no bananas*," Buster sang, done with the Help Wanted ads. He refolded the paper before offering it to Brian's father, who, in a way that made clear who had first rights to it, said that he'd seen it.

"If you're finished and you're going out," his father said, "find somebody to visit, but take some advice. Don't go up to Maxie's this early. There's a real bunch of young scrounges that hang around in there now, and they haven't got anything but long faces and a pool of change between them." He drew a long breath. "And you don't want that."

"Right," Brian said. He'd heard it all before, because the bars had once been a way of life for Uncle Buster. "The Shea family's concession to the alcoholic imperative," Brian's mother would tell them every morning after Buster had come home looped.

"*My canary has circles under his eyes*," Buster sang quietly.

"I think they all just wait there for your old pal Dandy," his father said.

"He still on with the ironworkers?" Brian asked. He was anxious to hear more of Dan Desmond, whom the nuns had called Dan D. because the first grade was full of Daniels that year.

"He is," said Buster.

"Jack Moore get on?"

"Jack Moore's a scrounge," his father said.

"No," said Buster. "I heard he was scrubbing down freezers at the Fish Pier. But that was a while ago. In Maxie's they don't wait for him anymore."

Good, Brian thought, no one even knew he was back and Jack Moore's was where he'd go to announce it. Jack would be at home. If nothing had changed in these last years, his good friend would still be in bed or up watching cartoons and waiting for Dandy to get off work. He got up with his plate in his hand.

"I'll take care of the dishes," Buster told him, "leave it."

Brian pulled out a wad of traveler's checks and fanned them with his thumb. "Gotta cash some of these," he told his father.

"Oh, we won't forget," Buster said. "Ten bucks, was it?"

Brian started for the bathroom.

"Your mother lost a back molar last week," his father called after him. "How much does she get for that?"

"See the tooth fairy, tell her."

"Or the cops," said Buster, straining to clear his throat of food, "—if it was your father put it out!"

Brian was quick with his shower.

"Take care now," his father said.

"Come again," said Buster.

＊　　＊　　＊

The Moores rented the top floor in a three-decker closeby. So that Brian wouldn't wake Mr. Moore, too, Jack moved him out onto his front porch, and went back in for the coffee. Brian tested the rail before resting his foot on it. In the past two years his friend, like the wild hedge below, had somehow overgrown himself. His voice had coarsened. And the droopy mustache was new. It looked full of weeds.

He watched two teenage boys shoulder one another against the tightly parked cars as they made their way down the opposite side of the street. Though he didn't recognize them, they were white, and thinking they were from the neighborhood he waved. "I'm back!" he wanted to holler, to anybody. But they were too busy horsing around. Like he and Jack and Dandy used to. He smiled. Maybe he should get Jack out running. What a walrus!

"How's your mother?" he asked when Jack returned.

"Everyone keeps expecting her to die and she keeps on working, I don't know." He lit a Camel.

The two in the street crossed and started back on the near side. Brian felt a nudge. Now he saw what Jack meant, the method in their horseplay, scanning the cars for something to snatch.

Jack pulled him away from the rail. He poured his coffee out into a large planter filled with dirt and doused his cigarette there. When they'd passed the house he heaved the empty cup at them, then jumped back with Brian, who could hear it shatter on the sidewalk.

"Why are we standing back here?" Brian asked.

"Hey, you never know with these little pricks. You go out for a beer and they bust half your windows. Let em guess where it come from." He lit another Camel.

"Broke a good cup." Brian couldn't think of anything else to say. He stepped up to the rail and watched them turn coolly into a side street. What a put off. There'd been thieves in the neighborhood before. But as open about it? He tried to remember how people used to take care of that.

"Hey," Jack said, "if I could've hefted the old lady's goddamn dead palm pot . . ."

Over more coffee they discussed the April evacuation of Vietnam and traded like baseball cards the two years of stories since

Brian's last leave home. When a pale man named McDonough came by they loaded a cooler with ice and grapefruit juice and moved downstairs to the front steps. Jack cracked the fifth of tequila he'd fetched earlier, with Brian's money.

"Let's have a drink together," he'd said.

"On me," Brian had insisted, but all he'd had was the wad of twenty-dollar traveler's checks.

"Not to worry," Jack had told him. "You sign it, they know me, I'll cash it."

Brian moved to the foot of the long wooden steps.

"You don't have to sit practically on the damn sidewalk," Jack said. "Come up here where we can still look down on people."

"There's somebody living there," Brian said, pointing up at the windows of the first-floor apartment.

"No." Jack shook his head tiredly, like he was dealing with a child. "No. There's some old couple in there. And they're either deaf, pick one, or they're always off in Baltimore with a married son."

"But I come by and we can't stay in the house anymore," McDonough said. His eyes took in the hammock slung across a shady corner of Jack's third-story porch.

"I was afraid the old man'd wake up and think this was his," Jack said, raising the bottle.

And they were in a better position now to try sweet talking the young nurses who hurried in pairs among the neighborhood's several hospitals, or to ogle some smartly dressed woman in for a visit. Over whose shiny Mercedes, or Volvos, or Buicks they were, after all, doing a kind of guard duty. Brian was feeling high again, and even McDonough, whom he didn't know well, seemed genuinely pleased to have him back.

"Let's head up to Maxie's soon," Brian said. "On me."

"On *me*," Jack said. "I've still got the change from your traveler's check here. Did you want that back?"

"Keep it."

"After, we'll all go up to Maxie's. Welcome home first."

They drank to that.

"So did you do anything over there?" McDonough wanted to know.

"In the Aleutians?" It was answer enough, even for McDon-

ough, a slow case. Do anything? Sure he had. He'd got stuck
with a low number in one of the last Selective Service lottery
drawings and promptly enlisted. That or the draft. With his de-
cent test scores he'd been guaranteed easy duty, a noncombat
unit, although enlistment had added an extra year to his tour.
His number was never called. The draft ended. For three years
he did exactly what he'd set out to do, and that was as little as
possible. Dummy, he thought. It wouldn't have been half so bad
if they'd just sent him someplace warmer. South America, say.

"I had a cist on the end of my spine," McDonough said, "and
they told me they couldn't draft me till I got it off."

"All I saw was this flaky corporal from ordnance who used to
shoot gulls with an old carbine out behind the armory," Brian
said.

McDonough wasn't listening. "Maybe I should've," he said.

Jack waved down a distracted-looking man whom Brian had
mistaken for an outpatient at the Mental Health Center in the
next block. Brian shook hands with Maxie's new bartender, a
Greek who called him "sir" and trotted off toward Huntington
Avenue.

"Dandy walks in Maxie's at four forty-five," Jack said, as he
and McDonough appeared to synchronize their watches. "He'll
be very glad to see you, Brian."

He'd be glad to see Dandy, too. They'd been close. And he
had a rough feeling now, a thing nipping just at the heels of his
party mood, that maybe he'd have more fun with somebody
who had two nickels to rub together.

                    *   *   *

At Maxie's he couldn't buy a round, so thrilled was Dandy to
see him back. He was relieved to see Dandy in his work boots
and dungarees and dirty T-shirt, looking fit and bronzed.

If not for his caution earlier with the tequila, Brian was sure
he'd be legless. So many of his friends were there. He stood
in the bright light of the bar and admired the highbacked old-
fashioned booths with their mahogany finish, and listened to
Tommy Kayne, who was telling him about Junior Farrell. Junior
had gone out to Oklahoma for no reason at all and got arrested

and been made to leave the state. It was as simple as that, Tommy said.

"And then, the way home, he hits on this big blond chick in the back of the bus and they get it on all the way to Mission Hill. He's still got her at his place."

"Locked up good and tight?" Brian asked.

"No," Dandy said, "pregnant."

For a second time Brian had to hear from someone about the night when Hump Munga used another man as an ax to batter all the video games in the café across the street, after losing a bet.

"How's your sister Rita, by the way?" McDonough asked on the heels of that story. Or he was still digesting the one about the blond from Oklahoma.

"She's in night school," Brian said, wondering at the same time why it wasn't enough just to say she worked days behind the beauty counter at Jordan Marsh.

"My sister goes to college," Jack said.

"So?" said McDonough. "Both my cousins went. Carol and what's-her-name."

"My mother was once engaged to the nephew of the president of Ecuador," Brian said. "Met him in a dance class she was teaching at the Roxbury YWCA. She was only eighteen years old."

"Think where you'd be today," Dandy said. "A prince."

Brian lowered his voice. "Except she missed the boat. My grandmother told her she'd have all these little 'pickaninnies.'"

"Still . . ." said Dandy.

By nine o'clock Brian had had his hand pumped by a dozen of his own acquaintances and several of his father's, and been kissed by two veteran waitresses who'd come over from the attached delicatessen to deliver sandwiches at the bar.

"Not many women in on a weeknight," Dandy told him. "Just Betty." A barrel-chested woman of about forty sat drinking beer in a circle of men at the end of the bar. "Interested?"

Brian realized that he'd been staring at Jeanie, the young bar waitress, who was bent suggestively over the jukebox. When she turned he was able to hold her eye an instant. Her face seemed flattened by a lack of expression, yet there was something vaguely fashionable in the full, perm-look of her copper hair and in the loose black skirt that brushed her calves as she moved about the booths. Her arms filled the short sleeves of her jersey and her nipples showed through the yellow cotton like the misplaced buttons of some undergarment. She conveyed a sense of fullness that aroused him. Seeing her stop a minute with the two waitresses from the deli, both in institutional whites and sturdy shoes with laces, Brian thought of an army exam question that involved selecting the one item that didn't fit in a given series.

She left the bar with three men, smiling at Brian as she passed. These were men well up in their twenties, and though they were white, he didn't know them.

"Two of the Dekker brothers," Dandy told him. "Which two, don't ask me. Must be a dozen of them around and they all look like that."

Both brothers were in high spirits, and each wore a bright nylon shirt open to the slight bulge just below his perfectly smooth chest. Their thick black hair was styled to fit around their heads like a lacquered cap. Brian couldn't help thinking of the half-crazy Italian barber his uncle had so enjoyed taking him to as a boy. "Cut the hair to the shape of the shoe!" he'd say.

"And the ratty-looking guy is Stevie Cole," Dandy said.

"Wait," Jack said. "The Dekker with the limp is the hero Dekker. He'll tell you. He got behind a guy who got behind a guy who stepped on a land mine. But christ, did those little buggers pay!"

Jeanie held the door for the man, one of whose legs Brian could now see was shorter than the other, but who seemed happy.

"She with him?" Brian asked.

Jack just looked at him. "Who worries about a guy you can take?" he said.

"They went out to smoke a joint," Dandy said, "that's all. Too many cops in and out of the deli."

"Check your uncle," Jack said.

Brian saw Buster pass slowly by the bar's long window, looking in. They waved and he smiled back. Then he appeared to
sing something, mouthing the words for Brian's benefit. When
Brian shook his head he did it again.

"What in the christ?" Jack said.

"Aha!" Brian snapped his fingers in the air. "*The bear missed
the train and now he's walkin'?*"

Buster nodded silently. Another of his favorites. Brian smiled,
the others laughed, and Buster lumbered off toward the green
benches on Brigham Circle, where he joined a small group of
men older than himself.

Jack turned to Brian and smiled crookedly. "You should tell
that old nun to get in here off his wagon and buy a round."
Brian reddened.

"Don't be so sensitive," Jack told him.

Brian took a long swallow of his beer so that he wouldn't
have to answer. It wasn't Buster he was sensitive about. It was
Jack himself, and how he'd been sounding all day. Like some
smart-assed army card sharp.

The Greek bartender Brian had met outside Jack's house was
talking to Dandy about "vanles."

"Vanles?" said Dandy. "Don't talk to me about vanles. Some
whiz stole the plaque with all the names." He nodded in the
direction of the large stone put on the Circle after World War II
to honor the neighborhood's dead.

"Bronze gone up in the market?" Brian said to no one in par-
ticular, aware at once that he'd sounded just like Jack. He
turned away from the others and as if on cue, a short, bubble-
like man dashed in the door.

"Can't stay away?" Jack said.

"Sure sure," Maxie told him, "I should walk your dog?"

He had thick arms and slickered black hair that fought thinning. He wore wire-rim bifocals and baggy black pants, a narrow belt, and a white shirt with the sleeves rolled and the neck
open. During Prohibition he was supposed to have run whiskey
with his brother Abe, an ex-wrestler who ran the deli counter
now and shaved his head. Maxie's was a way of life. At Christmas he'd give his best customers a half pint of Old Thompson,

which Uncle Buster said was cheap but thoughtful of him. Brian remembered his mother's letter about Maxie coming to visit Grandfather Hines's deathbed just before the priest.

Waving an apron that would hang to his ankles, Maxie took over the bar. Brian shook hands goodnight with the polite Greek, whose fear that Maxie might get wind of it had kept him from setting up a round in Brian's honor. First Jack and then Dandy and McDonough had joined in badgering the man, who'd been even more embarrassed than Brian.

"Hey!" Maxie hollered at Jack. "Who's this one?"

Brian extended his hand over the bar and Maxie locked it in both of his.

"A Shea?" he asked.

"Right," said Brian. "Brian Shea."

"I knew your grandfather," he said, still with Brian's hand. "Sure, and your father. And your mother. A beautiful woman! She ate on the other side. 'Red' I called her. Your Uncle Buster. Ah, your uncle. I could tell you. But they're well?" Brian said they were. "Aunts and uncles on your Hines side I knew. So many." Maxie's voice had grown wistful. He released the hand. "Way before you," he called back as he went to fill an order.

From a near booth a slim black man in a green hospital top hollered "Bullshit!" to someone's claim of seven aces. Tommy Kayne was in the game. And Junior Farrell. Brian had seen it played in the army. They had one dollar bills in place of cards and were using the serial numbers to bluff bids. Liar's poker. McDonough had been kibitzing, and now both he and Jack wanted to play. They pleaded with Dandy to give them a ten-dollar bill so they could break it into singles and double what they called his investment.

"Go away," Dandy said.

"Hang on," Brian told them.

"They'll just lose it," Dandy said.

But Brian hadn't been able to buy a round all night. It was time he paid for something.

"Great," said Jack.

McDonough eyed the black men clustered at the booth. "Got

a good thing on over there with some of the hospital help," he said under his breath.

Brian pulled out the doubled-over wad of traveler's checks. "Never got to the bank," he said absently. "Max!"

Before Brian could say anything more, Maxie was telling him how, twenty-five years ago, "Your father was dating your mother who lived on some street then. Now there's the Project." He made a noise with his lips and went on. Even Jack was listening. Maxie gestured to the streetcar tracks beyond his window on Huntington Avenue.

"The trolley didn't run so late and your father he'd come in when he missed it. Stand where you stand now. And your Grandfather Hines in the mornings, but he always sits, he's old he thinks. That's another time. So about your father, he's standing and waiting for Max to close. Maybe a hundred times. Here we go half across town in the middle of the night to South Boston, in my car, so he can sleep in his own bed. Get married to that girl and have a Brian Shea I told him, because I have to keep my doors locked and the windows up driving into there you understand. Even with your father, a battler. Sure." He rolled his eyes in the direction of the men in the game.

"Who knows from blacks then? A lot of thick micks, I'm sorry, but those days they'd be just as happy to nab a Maxie."

"Or an Abie," Abe said. This was something, since Abe seldom left the deli counter and only talked in food orders. Down the bar someone tittered. Brian raised his packet of checks.

"Can you dance?" Maxie cried. "Your mother could dance!"

"And I could be a prince now," Brian cried back. He tore off one of the checks and held it up for Maxie's inspection.

"What's this?"

"Need a little cash."

"No checks."

"Traveler's checks?"

"The rules."

Without a hint of apology Maxie dipped into the beer chest and presented Brian with a bottle of Narragansett.

"Where's mine?" Jack wanted to know.

"You're here, he's not," said Maxie, turning up his palms with a shrug.

"Well he was drinking Budweiser!" Jack hollered after him.

One lousy traveler's check. Brian felt mildly humiliated, then altogether angry.

"See Leon," Dandy told him. "Go and cash it in the drugstore. Leon'll take care of it."

Outside, Jeanie was sitting barefoot on the hood of a car. The smallest of the men with her, Stevie Cole, was holding one of her platform sandals under his nose. He had the face of a man who was looking for something to snatch. He pretended to be overcome and passed the sandal to her, and she was putting it on as Brian walked by.

"That's just the new-car smell," Brian told her. "They spray that in."

The other two (Dekker, was it?) smiled stiffly, but when Jeanie, in a warm voice, said "Hi," Stevie Cole narrowed his eyes unmistakably. Brian hadn't been away so long he'd forgotten that around here that sort of thing often ended in a fight, but he'd had a lot to drink and was pleased with the effect he was having on Jeanie. Anyway, he'd spent these last years in safety. Why should he expect to come home and enjoy the same privilege? He continued on to the drugstore, where Leon Friedman, the pharmacist, welcomed him home and cashed five twenty-dollar traveler's checks.

When he came out Jeanie was gone. In the bar he slipped Jack twenty more dollars, McDonough five, and cursed Maxie.

"Forget it," Dandy told him.

One of the Dekkers was at the jukebox. He saw it was the short-legged one. The second brother wasn't in the bar. Brian watched Jeanie begin to dance awkwardly with the man, then looked around for Stevie Cole.

"You got it made," Dandy comforted him.

Morning walks and bedroom talks, oh how I loved you then . . . Jim Croce sang.

"Another night." Dandy winked. "I can tell. And she's all yours."

"What other night?" Brian asked sharply. He had half a mind

to go and spend his money someplace else. He felt out of place; yet he wanted to dance. Dandy got another round.

Tommy Kayne and Junior Farrell were cleaned out of the game. From the sound of it, McDonough would be, too.

"Next Jack'll lose it all," Dandy said flatly. "Those people know how to bullshit, and that's the name of the game."

"Let's move on," Brian said.

"Where?"

"Anywhere."

"This is the best place right here," Dandy said. "It's just there's not many women in on a weeknight. Wait'll Friday. You get these Nova Scotian girls that all come into The Hitching Post to dance. Some nice stuff. For right now this is okay for me. What'll you do somewheres else? Watch guys fall off their stool? See a brawl? Hey! Brian?"

Brian had moved away from the bar. "I'm leaving," he yelled to Jack, who looked up distractedly from his game.

"Take care," Jack said.

"Yeh, take care," Dandy said. "You okay?"

"I'm okay," Brian said.

Some goodbye. Out on the sidewalk he tried to clear his head. He couldn't go home. It was too early to crash on the couch. The TV was in the living room and everybody would be up watching it. Reluctantly, he talked himself into a drink. There was no traffic. A few old men sat on the Circle benches in the distance. Was Buster still over there? He started across the avenue toward The Calumet Café.

"So your mother was a hoofer," someone called into the night. A second man laughed. So now everyone knew. He wouldn't much care if Maxie had just cashed the damn check.

He stepped ahead, drawn to the streetcar tracks that may have taken his Grandfather Hines the last leg from County Cork, or his mother the first few blocks to Ecuador, but now only divided the space between a bar and a café. Stopping in the middle of the avenue, he turned back toward Maxie's, to the doorway where Stevie Cole and the other Dekker were just emerging.

"My mother could dance," he said. "That's right."

Dekker drew close. "Stay away from my brother's girl," he said.

"Okay," Brian said. He didn't care. He only wanted to go somewhere else.

Dekker looked puzzled. He began to back off, a car horn blasted, and then Stevie Cole, who looked like he had to do something, tried to give Brian a parting shove. Brian grabbed his arm and threw him on the ground. Dekker swung. The punch landed on Brian's shoulder, but in stepping away from it he caught his foot in the track and fell hard on his knees. Something snapped that hurt like hell. His ankle burned. He looked up to see a car move slowly around Stevie Cole, who had his foot poised for the kick. Kick! He didn't care. There was too much pain. He began to crawl away between the rails. No one kicked him.

Some men came out to him. A taxi slowed and the driver hollered to get off of the road. Then he heard Buster's voice.

"Come on, Brian," he said. He put his big hand on Brian's shoulder. "Let's get you up."

Still on his hands and knees, Brian glanced up at Buster, then down the length of the track. He began again to crawl, dragging the killing ankle.

"Come on, boy," Buster said. "You'll hurt yourself worse. What are you doing down there?"

"Crawling to Ecuador," Brian said between his teeth.

Buster was silent a moment. "Well," he said then, "don't you think we should tell the folks?"

"You do it."

Buster didn't say anything more as he walked slowly along beside him.

BLOOD

Her jeans were laundered to the barest blue and she wore a white T-shirt that said Antonio's Nuthouse Bar on the front, which most of the men they passed in the street tried to read. He wore a dark flannel jacket buttoned to the neck of his thermal undershirt. They held hands with their fingers interlocked. When the sun looked like it might stay out, she made him stop and unbuttoned his jacket. People in the Monday lunch rush made room for them.

She stroked his chest with her newspaper, which was neatly folded to Apartment Rentals.

"I'm glad you came along, Brian," she said. "It helps. Thanks. You're sweet."

"Just 'sweet'?" he said. "Last night what was it you said I was?"

"Well, but that was night," she said, "and this is day. It's like meeting you all over again. We've never done anything together in the daylight."

"So how am I doing?"

"You're sweet," she said.

They stopped again, as if to consider what they might want in that crowd.

"My hematology professor has his practice in that building," she said.

There was a shiny brass knocker on the building's oak door and a plaque in the bricks beside it. Brian glanced up at the windows on the top floor.

"I've heard the best place to find apartments is in a Laundromat," he said.

"I'd almost rather live in a Laundromat. Anything to be out of that group house. One of them taped a note last week to my sugar bowl, 'White Death' with a big X. You know you may be the only normal person I've met there all year."

"It was a nice party."

"Somebody told me you were one of Tom's friends, which didn't seem to fit, but Tom told me Susan had just sort of met you out walking in the street. As far as I'm concerned, it was a point in your favor not knowing any of them."

"They seem like nice people."

"I think they all sense that you're a meat-eater. But tell me where you heard this about Laundromats?"

"Oh, from some painter or other. What you do is check the bulletin boards."

"Know it all, those painters." She half turned to look at him. "Is that what you do, paint?"

"Lately," he said.

"I'm sorry. It's like ever since we met I've kept up all this nervous chatter about me, that horrible house, school. I just never thought to ask what else you did when you were out of work. I don't know what you do when you do work. You have to understand, Brian, that my winter was all books and no play. Would you tell me if I was sounding too self-involved?"

"No," he said.

"You're sweet to listen. It's your fault."

"I'll try not to listen to you," he said.

She pulled his arm closer to her side. He kissed her hair.

"What I know about medicine you could fit in a thimble," he said. "Never ran into a medical student before. You're a lot more interesting than what I could tell you."

"But you paint," she said. "That's wonderful. And it begins to explain you. Aren't painters all supposed to be out of work, lean, and handsome, just a bit abstracted?"

"Painters?"

"Of course painters. Is there enough light, are you able to work where you are?"

"When it pays."

"Someone pays you?"

"I hope so."

"Wait," she said. "Something tells me we're not talking about painting paintings."

Brian shrugged. "Baby, I've worked with guys that would paint anything," he said.

She smiled off into the crowd, the traffic, beyond it. "Well," she said, "at least now I know what you do, some of the time."

"You do," he said.

She raised her newspaper. "Do we look into another one of these, or do we think about lunch?"

"You really don't like any of the places we've seen so far?"

"Brian," she said.

"There was one that had some light coming in, didn't it?"

"From the air shaft."

"No, you're right. You're the one who has to live in it."

"But I want to know what you think."

"I might've taken it," he said. "For the money."

"Well, there's that. The important thing is that it be bright, and I can have people over—you, for example—without tip-toeing around a lot of right-living-whatever-they-ares in that house. Harvard Medical's own Gang of Four.—Would you?"

"Stay over?"

"Yes."

"I could help you with your homework."

"Homework, really. That would be nice too."

"Memorize bones."

"So why don't I buy us lunch? We're celebrating." She spread her arms. "Daylight saving time."

"My turn," he said.

"No," she said.

"I didn't bring anything for your party last night."

"Nobody asked you to. And you made me breakfast."

"They were your eggs."

"Don't be silly."

She pulled him closer and though he smiled at her his expression didn't seem to change.

"Okay," she said, "be silly. Your turn. But I wish you wouldn't feel that way."

Brian pointed out a deli on the other side of the street. "Go on over there," he said, resting his hands on her shoulders, "and get us a booth. Order some coffee, you know, soup, a sandwich, whatever you feel like. Just don't try and pay for anything, because I'll be right back."

"Sounds like a plan."

"Half an hour. Got an appointment." He nodded into the distance.

"Half an hour?"

"Just go ahead and order and I'll be right back."

She looked into the same distance. "Where's your appointment?"

"In that direction. Mission Hill."

"I'd really almost rather go along."

"Twenty-five, thirty minutes. No more."

"I wouldn't mind, really."

Both appeared to consider the distance. Finally she looked down at her newspaper.

"Mission Hill. Is that where you live?"

"In that direction," he said.

"Have you lived there long?"

"Born there. Still there."

"There are some very reasonable rentals there."

"You don't want them, Lynn."

"I guess not," she said.

                    *   *   *

Though there was no answer he continued jabbing the buzzer marked MOORE, then sailed back out of the lobby of the Mission Park housing tower. The sun had gone in again and he buttoned his jacket before crossing the avenue to Burke's. Jack Moore, Stevie Cole, and a man in his thirties called Crepes stood out on the sidewalk in front of the open bar door.

"Jack," Brian called from the street, "I was just over ringing your bell."

"I'm not in," Jack said. "You should've called."

"Your phone's disconnected."

"Is that what happened to it?" Jack said.

"How's it going, Brian?" asked Crepes.

"Yeh, okay," Brian said distractedly. "How's your mother?"

Crepes's ruddy face drooped as he considered the question. "Still good for cigarette money," he said.

Brian closed on Jack Moore. "I'm in a bind," he said. "Can you let me hold twenty for a couple of days? Ten if that's all you can do right now."

Jack laughed and put his arm around Brian's shoulders. He put his lips close to Brian's ear. "If I had twenty bucks," he said, "I'd be in at the bar instead of out here with the unwashed."

"This is completely aside from whatever you owe me, Jack. I'm not even asking for that now. I'll get the full thing back to you."

"I got cigarette money, Brian, come on." His voice rose. "I'm waiting for my brother to get off work so I can hit him up. See me then."

"I need it now. I left someone, this Lynn, she's in a deli in Kenmore Square. I'm supposed to pay for lunch. I don't have bus fare."

"Lynn?"

"I hit a party last night. She's a medical student."

"You're fantastic."

Brian lowered his voice. "This is a little different," he said.

"You bet."

"I thought yesterday was your unemployment check?"

"Them are all run out, Brian. Listen to me. Go back and tell her hey. You got a knack. Who knows? Broads are crazy. College broads."

"College broads," Stevie Cole said. He humped the air.

"See what you started," Brian said to Jack.

"I'll tell you your problem, Shea," Stevie Cole said. "You're about half smart, you know?"

"Hey hey hey," Jack said. He stepped between them. "See what *you* started," he said to Brian. "What for?"

"What's your problem, man?" Stevie said. His voice cracked.

Brian put his hands up with his palms open. "I'm leaving," he said.

Crepes stepped toward him and with a quick, jerky motion

pulled out his wallet. "What kind of blood have you got?" He handed Brian a card.

"Crepes!" Jack said.

Brian eyed the card. "'O,'" he said.

"See?" Crepes said. He looked at Jack. "Don't piss on the un-washed. You're 'O,'" he said to Brian, "I'm 'O.' That's my card there. I'm all registered, it's just I'm in no shape. You're okay, right? Let her flow. Twenty bucks a pint."

Again Brian examined the card. "I can just go in, like that?"

"You never done this?" Crepes said.

"Twenty bucks," Jack said. "Do it."

"Where do I go?"

"Not the Brigham," Crepes said. "They know me there. Do the Deaconess. You got the card, right? Same blood, you're as good as being me."

"She gonna wait?" Jack said.

Brian looked aside a moment to where his reflection caught in the bar window, then turned back smiling. "Wouldn't you?" he said.

"Tell her you got hung up. You watch, she'll believe it," he winked at Crepes. "Bum's luck."

"Bum's luck," Stevie Cole muttered.

"Ten minutes to get there," Crepes said, "the whole thing won't take half an hour."

"Shea's probably scared of needles," Stevie Cole said, but he was leaning against the front of the bar now with his hands in his pockets. He might have been talking about someone who wasn't there.

"Hey, Crepes, thanks," Brian said.

"Just don't lose the card."

"The Deaconess Hospital?"

"Sixth floor," Crepes said. He and Jack drifted out to the curb to watch Brian run.

*   *   *

The elevator light in the lobby hung at five. Brian took the stairs two at a time. At the sixth-floor landing he found a room where a nurse took the donor card Crepes had given him.

"You better sit down," she said. "I wouldn't dare take your blood pressure yet."

He flopped into one of the plastic chairs along the wall and undid his jacket. A younger nurse came out of another room then and stood over him. Her uniform skirt fell above her knees. She wore high white socks and Nikes with oversized soles. Briam remained slouched in the chair, drawing long breaths.

"Ready?" he said.

"What'd you have in mind?" she said.

The nurse who'd taken his card laughed from across the room. There were two other men in the row of chairs but neither nurse paid them any attention.

"Mr. McKenna?" she said.

Brian looked puzzled. He straightened up in his chair.

"It's okay," she said, "I know it's you." She glanced at the other two men. "Mathematically."

"It really is," he said. "I'm a little out of it."

"That's the way I like them," she said to the older nurse in a voice like Mae West's. "Just step into my office and I'll, ah, prick your finger for you." Everyone but Brian laughed this time.

"I'll need a drop of your blood for my test tube," she said. "How about it?"

Brian followed her into the other room and sat in another plastic chair.

"I'll bet by now you could do all this yourself," she said, her eye on the dog-eared card on the table.

He hurriedly took off his jacket and rolled up the sleeve of his thermal undershirt so that she could take his blood pressure.

"Did you actually run up all those stairs?"

"I did."

"Remarkable," she said. "Pressure's normal. Let's have the finger."

She pricked his index finger, extracting a drop of blood that she let fall into a thin tube of liquid. They watched it gently hover about a third of the way down.

"A watched pot never boils," she said.

"There it goes."

"It's supposed to drop like a rock."

"It did, at the end."

"It's nothing," she said. "Low iron. Eat a steak. But do come back and see us, by all means."

"I can't," Brian said. He let the gauze pad fall from his finger and with his thumb forced out another drop of blood. "Let's give it another shot."

"Really, no," she said. "I'm afraid that would be silly."

Brian smiled broadly. "I know," he said, his finger out.

"I really wish you wouldn't be this way."

She hesitated, then extracted another droplet from the finger. Together they watched the blood hover in the tube.

"We could wait," she said, "but it won't matter."

"I know, I know that."

"Sorry," she said.

He sat back slowly.

"How badly do you need the money?"

Brian looked up at her as if to say he'd just now thought about it. She leaned back on the table and crossed her ankles, again eyeing the donor card. When she spoke she smiled and her tone was light.

"What would you do with it anyway?"

"You're right," he said.

"Next time."

He looked up at her.

"Okay, but how far would twenty dollars have gotten you?"

"Lunch, maybe."

"That's not far, Mr. McKenna."

"Shea," he said. "But you're right." Brian sat forward with his arms on his knees. "It's not," he said, watching his blood in the tube like a man who has nothing but time.

WHOM GOD HATH PROMISED

There were two black men in the hallway when Walter came downstairs. One was installing a padlock on the door of the vacant first-floor apartment, the other smoking a joint. The one who was smoking straightened up and cupped the joint close against the front of his khaki workshirt.

"Very suspicious out," he said to Walter. He pointed at the man who was working. HARVARD CORPORATION was stitched in red on the back of his khaki shirt. "Rain, he thinks." Walter nodded, and they both watched the man work.

The smell of the joint filled the hallway. Still nodding his head, Walter pulled open the heavy outer door. Rain, he thought. He stepped cautiously out onto his front steps with the door pushing tight against his back.

Myles and Tea Kearney were on the steps watching the sidewalk.

"Hey, what time is it?" Walter asked. "I said what time is it?"

"You make us piss in the alley while you sit upstairs but you can't look at a clock?" Myles said. He was sitting on the top step, hunched over his knees. His narrow shoulders made his head look much bigger than it was, and the way he was sitting made Walter think he might suddenly topple to the sidewalk under the weight of it.

"My bathroom isn't a hangout," Walter said. "Just my stairs."

"What were you doing up there all by yourself, anyway?"

"Waiting for love to call," Walter said, which seemed to tickle Myles. Some joke. If he didn't square things soon with the phone company . . . The old wooden stairtreads gave under his sneakers as he stepped down to the sidewalk. He heard Kearney behind him shifting his bulk.

"I'll take one myself," Kearney said.

Walter took the last two bottles of beer from the Styrofoam cooler on the sidewalk. He pressed one to either side of his widow's peak. Once he was over the feeling that he wanted to be there, he could leave. The freezing glass stung his scalp. In August he'd be twenty-eight. All the Donnellys named Walter went bald early. More room for the brain to grow. Or it was a sign of virility, the way his mother used to tell it.

"So. What time is it?" he asked.

"Right," said Kearney. "That time again! I think we're dry." He shifted his bulk again to glare at Myles. "Who's gonna spring?"

Myles stepped gingerly down onto the sidewalk and examined the empty cooler.

"Goddammit, Walter," Kearney said. An unlit Lucky Strike bobbed between his lips. "I get one of those beers or what?"

"They're clearing my head."

"Well make it snappy, okay. Stevie Cole's old lady come by just now and she seen we had beer. So expect Stevie."

"Shit," said Myles.

"Look at it from her point of view," Kearney said. "Wouldn't you want him outdoors? He's only housebroke on newspapers."

Then Walter saw him. "He's here," he said.

"Gimme a smoke, Tea," Stevie said as soon as he was close enough to be heard without hollering.

Kearney, watching Myles, took out his cigarettes. "You springing or what?"

"How is it my turn?" Myles asked weakly.

Kearney's jaw as it dropped made four chins. "You're self-employed, aren't you? Of course it's your turn."

"Plus you're the one with the capital." Stevie Cole has spoken, Walter said to himself. Stevie's hair hung in muddy-looking clusters over his ears. Walter's mother had pegged his look years ago. A boy fleeing demons.

"Whose fault is that?" said Myles, who worked for himself as a housepainter. Which as often as not was a nice way to get out of working, Walter thought.

The two maintenance men came out of the hallway.

"What's this?" Stevie looked sidelong at them.

"Padlocked the first floor," Kearney told him.

"Know the time?" Walter asked the one who'd had the joint.

"*Over*time," he said.

Stevie cocked his head. "My man, you didn't put no padlock on that top floor, didja? Walter be upset. How's he gonna get in ol' Sylvie's, tear out a ceiling?"

"Sylvie?" Myles said. "Hey Walter. Not Sylvia? That true?"

Walter sipped his beer, watching the two black men unlock the rear doors of a Harvard Corporation van and stack their tools. How old *was* Sylvie? Forty? And then some. Anyhow, Stevie was only guessing.

Myles turned to Kearney. "Yesterday was Walter's unemployment check. Ask him to spring."

"That all goes for back union dues," Walter said. "Never mind the Sunday crossword."

Myles hesitated. "I'll give you the money," he told Kearney, "okay. Okay, but I don't wanna go for it."

Walter tossed a beer to Kearney. He knew Kearney wasn't going. He'd come by with a buzz on looking for the General Help section of last Sunday's paper, which Walter usually put aside for him. Myles had come too. But Walter had just been out running. He was closing in on a hundred and sixty pounds and hadn't wanted a drink. So they'd borrowed his paper, his cooler, and his beer and gone down on the steps, and now they'd attracted Stevie Cole. Walter guessed no one was going to ask Stevie to go for it. He kept a .25 caliber automatic hidden in a jungle boot next to his bed. Kearney lived right above him and told everyone that when Stevie was drunk enough he used the closet door in his own bedroom for target shooting. Kearney knew all about Stevie's wife, too.

"I don't hear a lot of violence down there," he'd told Walter last night at the bar in Burke's, "but she goes around like she's goddamn scared of him."

"Who wants to get shot?" Walter had said.

"I never really talked to her, but I figure she'd have to be dumb as a rock to be Stevie's wife. Wouldn't you know she'd be good-looking."

"Tough break for us," Walter had told him. "Now we'll have to take action." Yet there were times when he met her out pushing the stroller that he imagined Stevie's wife asking for his help. He wanted to believe, if she ever did ask, that he'd break Stevie's back for her. He was always relieved when their conversations began and ended on the same howdy-do.

Stevie swung his head and the muddy-looking strands on one side fell back behind his ear. "I'll make the next run," he said.

"Okay then," Myles said. "But Piels this time. One sixty-nine a sixpack on sale, cans. That's seven . . . eighty. Six eighty. Seventy-six. Six seventy-six a what? A case, right?"

"Right," said Kearney.

"Weren't we drinking Schlitz?" Stevie said.

"That was just a teaser," Kearney told him, and Myles set off down the block, alternating between a walk and a self-conscious jog in the direction of the Epicure Package Store.

"It's really beautiful out," Walter said. "What time is it now?"

"Ice!" Kearney hollered. "Get ICE!"

"Seven, eight o'clock," Stevie said.

"You going somewhere?" Kearney asked.

"Somewhere else. Wanna go?"

"You bet," said Kearney, which to Walter meant No, I'm drinking right here, and don't ask me again.

Stevie looked deep in thought. Please Jesus, Walter prayed, don't let him be weighing my offer to Kearney to go someplace else. Then he saw the girl Stevie was watching. She had on a white elastic tube top that she quickly tugged up under one arm when she saw them all staring. Too close now to fool with the other breast, she dropped her hand to the waistband of her cut-offs and walked faster. She was very young. Her breasts looked like the only finished part of her. Stevie wouldn't let that pass without comment. Walter moved casually out of her way on the sidewalk and stood in front of Stevie, who couldn't seem to find the words. Yellow down glistened in the hollow of her spine. She was three houses away before Stevie, digging into his shirt pocket, broke the silence.

"I had a joint," he said, "which I don't know where it is now."

"Check in your wallet," Kearney said.

Stevie inspected the crushed joint. "This is g-o-o-d shit," he told Kearney.

Walter watched him light up, then drained the last flat ounce of beer from the neck of his bottle. He looked around for the plastic trash bag he'd made Myles and Kearney take down with them. Glass sparkled in the weedy outline of a foundation next door. Walter spit hard into the gutter. In bars, Kearney drank from the bottle because the water they used to wash beer glasses wasn't hot enough to kill bacteria, he said. Myles was no better. He'd pack his van with old paint pots and drop cloths, but you wouldn't see a McDonald's wrapper or an empty Schlitz can in there. And Stevie. He'd never been friendly enough with the man to know if he had any clean habits at all.

"Where's the bag I gave you to bring down?" he asked irritably.

"We used it, we used it," Kearney said. "It's there behind your—" He looked at the thorn bushes in front of the house as if he'd never seen them before. "Garden," he said, relighting the joint.

Stevie began laughing to himself. Walter settled his bottle in the bag with the rest of the empties. It was starting to get dark, and he left quietly.

*   *   *

Myles, walking unevenly, appeared out of the shadow of the Medical Area power plant at the bottom of Francis Street.

"I should've drove," he said, "but Julie-from-up-at-Burke's, right?" He caught his breath. "I give her the keys to my van."

Walter helped him switch the outsized-looking case of beer to his other shoulder.

"You going down to The Winsor?" he asked, but Walter was already several steps closer to The Winsor Café and only waved goodbye.

"Write if you get work," Myles called after him.

Walter stepped lightly past the plant's three-hundred-foot smokestack. The young nurse he'd seen last week in The Winsor hadn't been much out of his thoughts. She'd been at a table

with some other hospital people. Walter was sitting with Tea
Kearney at the bar, idly lighting matches. He watched her group
get up to leave.

"You must be a pyromaniac," she'd said as she passed him,
then stopped and blew out his match.

"Pyro*phile*," said one of the men with her, and she'd walked
to the door laughing. Kearney was still staring after them with
his eyebrows raised when Walter heard another nurse call her
name. Amaris. She turned sharply, and though the image was
now a week old, Walter had no trouble recalling the few inches
of bare flesh exposed between the hem of her uniform and her
white kneesocks.

He'd looked her up in one of his sisters' old books, *What To
Name the Baby?* "Amaris," it said: "'Whom God Hath Promised.' Hebrew. From the Biblical name Amariah." So she was
Jewish. Dynamite. Didn't opposites attract? He couldn't wait to
run into her again, he'd told Kearney.

"Good luck," Kearney had said out of the side of his mouth.
An overweight cherub, the Xaverian brother who taught their
Latin class used to call Kearney. He'd got so bloated he was
sour on everything now. Even Amaris, lying on her stomach beneath the ferns, the wandering jews and spider plants that made
a garden of her bedroom. She smiled. Semen was trickling from
the folds of her labia. Was that right? Walter decided yes, that
they'd already made love, and now she was reaching for the
white hand towel folded like a handkerchief on her nightstand.
He grabbed her arm and held her back. In the army whores always did that, he told her. That's your experience, she told him.
Was it ever right, he wondered.

His thoughts returned to Kearney. Who wasn't called Tea for
nothing. They'd served mass together in grade school until
an old priest whose name Walter couldn't remember caught
Kearney slugging altar wine. He was wild.

"That's why they call you 'Tea'?" he kept yelling. "Like your
'tea,' do you? That's why they call you 'Tea'? Do you suppose
Jesus had a nickname?"

"J-bird," Kearney seemed to say against his own will. Word of
it got everywhere, and from then on whenever he called at

the house Walter's mother made him wait out on the landing.
Walter's mother was dead now, so was his father. Whoever
wasn't dead had left. He had seven rooms of his own, no one to
run him out of the only bathroom, and Kearney was over all the
time, dammit.

Walter stood waiting for the pedestrian light at Longwood
Avenue. A young couple brushed past him and dodged hand in
hand through the traffic. Pedestrian light? Where in hell was he
going? An ambulance ran the light and sped down Brookline
Avenue toward the Beth Israel Hospital. He'd overshot The
Winsor by a good block. "Idiot," he mumbled.

His head wasn't on straight. He waited on the corner as if the
WALK light might tell him something, but then instead of crossing with it or turning back, he went right on Longwood. When
he met Amaris he wanted his head to be on straight. The Winsor could wait and some air was what he needed.

After the Children's Hospital Medical Center the sidewalks
were empty. Harvard Medical School spread off to his right.
Three black boys and a girl with a portable radio in her lap were
sitting on the stone wall where the school's long grass quad-
rangle met the street. The smooth white stone looked so old
and delicately cut he thought it must have been brought over.
Big as a case of twelve-ounce cans, that radio. Why weren't they
in under the lawn sprinklers? He and Kearney as kids, summer
nights, everyone used to get run out of there. He supposed
they'd be run off the wall, too, soon enough.

He passed the Lying-In Hospital, Harvard Dental School. No
telling how much the family had saved on him in there. But that
was a dim memory and coincided with one of an army barracks
where the rows of dentists' stations looked like so many barber
chairs. His father's front teeth were in a ceiling at Harvard University. He'd been over there on a laborer's job mixing plaster in
a tub, put a hose in his mouth for a drink, rinsed, spit some
water in the tub, and come home puzzled about the loss of his
partial plate. He liked to tell you it was up in a ceiling in Harvard Hall.

A good plasterer's story, Walter thought, he'd told it himself
many a time on one job or another. He remembered the old

man fondly, eating plateloads of smelts on a Friday night. Sometimes he'd talked about Harvard like he'd gone to it. Why not? He'd given them the best teeth in his head.

He was nearing the Massachusetts College of Pharmacy now, and Roxbury Community College at the corner of Huntington Avenue. The projects lay ahead. The safety island in the middle of the avenue was crowded with students waiting for the trolley. Left or right? A cabbie hit his brakes. As Walter waved him on, a tall white man in a sleeveless camouflage shirt raced up and threw his umbrella and briefcase into the back. He thought about driving a cab. Kearney had tried it. You had to hustle, naturally, and watch the back of your head. Six more days to his next unemployment check.

He passed the Harvard School of Public Health, the Countway Medical Library, full circle along the high concrete wall of the Brigham and Women's Hospital Complex. He was at the top of Francis Street. He'd left Tea, Myles, and Stevie Cole further down Francis Street on his front steps not a half hour ago. So much for going home. Ahead, The Chopping Block, The Circle Bar and Deli, The Hitching Post, Burke's. A trolley rattled past, and he crossed with the lights to Brigham Circle.

*   *   *

"Get in," the woman said through her clenched teeth. She stood squarely in the glass doorway. He'd got to South Huntington Avenue. Her flat white hair was bobby pinned so tightly to her head that he could see streaks of her scalp. A filmy housedress hung unevenly above her knees. Her arms were twice his, the face boiled and puffy. The little girl to whom she spoke was sitting with her feet dangling over the side of the low concrete stoop, her eyes on Walter. Her short black hair was just as lifeless, but she was too dark, too pretty to be the boiled woman's. He felt better. The girl scrambled off the stoop and the woman threw her into the hallway against a row of mailboxes. When he drew even with the stoop they were gone. On the next stoop three blacks in identical skintight T-shirts shook their heads sadly and tut-tutted at him in Spanish. So if she's white? he almost said to them.

"Hey, don't say nothing to the fat lady," a husky, woman's voice warned behind him. Walter spun around.

"I didn't," he said.

She was sitting in a bowfront window overlooking the stoop of the fat lady's building. In a simpler way she looked as good as Amaris had. He drew up to the sill.

"She broke my tooth, that lady." When Walter didn't answer she bared her teeth. "A front one," she said. She rubbed it. His hand moved automatically over the thirty-dollar stash in the front pocket of his dungarees. Her expression brightened then, her eyes following his movement. She spoke softly but faster, as if he were the simple one.

"I have a friend's a dentist. He fixed it like, you know, he fixed it. My friend. I have friends everywhere."

"I bet you do," Walter said airily. He wouldn't look like a mark. What was she? Half an Indian? Her shoulder-length hair was dark and straight like the girl's, but looked freshly washed and combed. Gypsy, he decided.

"Come in. Come inside, you." Walter stayed put. "You don't have to," she said. She smiled. "We can make a wish together."

"I don't think I need my driveway oiled right now, thank you," he said. Did she think he wasn't onto all the gypsy cons?

She looked startled. "My name's Marie," she said. "I don't do that, what you said."

"No no." He tried to laugh. What did she think he meant? "It's like banging dents out of your fenders." Her face went blank. "Fly-by-night jobs is what I meant," he said. "Like gypsies do. Your name's really Marie?" It sounded normal enough. Marie.

"You think I'm gypsy?"

"Naw." He felt less conspicuous. The three blacks had gone under the hood of an old Impala with their flashlights.

"What am I?"

He smiled. "Albanian."

"Albanian?" Street light shone on her bare arms, her hair, in her eyes, and she was smiling again.

"From Albany," he said.

"New York? You know New York City?"

"I don't. Shall we head down there?"

She laughed. "I been there already. Lots of times. All over New York. Times Square. Chicago. Birmingham." She glanced back into the room. "I have tea," she said abruptly, then flung her hand toward the three bent over the Impala. "Come in, *gadjo*, or those will strip you for parts."

When he turned again to the window she was gone. "Gadjo"? He didn't want to leave, but knew now was the time. She reappeared in the glassed hallway and held the outer door open for him.

"In in in," she said. She took his hand and led him through an inner glass door. To the right of the stairwell her apartment door stood open. Still holding his hand, she dropped the deadbolt.

"Dark." He hadn't noticed that from outside. Or much else above the sill except her face.

"By the windows," she said.

The shades were drawn tight on two of them, so that the only light came through the one in the curve of the bowfront where she'd been sitting. She sat him in an aluminum lawn chair at a small card table before stretching over the table to raise the shade on the middle window. She wore her short sleeves rolled. He could see the plain white blouse hadn't been ironed. Her army surplus pants fit the firm arc of her cheeks.

"Ah," Walter said. "Light."

The dark tablecloth resembled a tapestry. Two squat white candles were mounted there on the arms of a fancy cross.

"You Greek Orthodox?" he asked. He wondered did gypsies even have a religion.

She removed an empty teacup with a Red Rose teabag crushed in the plastic saucer and put it behind her on the sill, then repositioned the folding chair that had been at her window and sat opposite him. He fingered a wick.

"Gonna light these?"

"Only if you make a wish."

"What for?"

"You can make three wishes. For life, for love, for whatever you wish for. But keep one to yourself."

"This sounds like *The Third Secret*."

"You know The Third Wish?"

It sounded like the name of a child's game. Why shouldn't he know it? "'Secret,' I said. It goes like this. The first secret you tell a friend. The second one you only tell to yourself."

"And the third?"

"That's the secret," he said. "*The Third Secret*. Some movie."

"Only a movie? So. Now you tell me *your* secret."

"I don't have any secrets."

"No secret wish? You want something." She smiled. "I know you want something."

"Maybe. How about you?"

"Me? I don't wish for nothing."

"No no." He put his hands flat on the table. His lawn chair wobbled. "I meant I wanted you."

She lowered one arm onto the table. Thinking she wanted to hold his hand again, he gripped it. Suddenly she was on her feet. "Feel free to turn me down," he started to say, but then her chair folded with a crash. A light went on and an oily-looking man about Walter's age in a sleeveless undershirt told him to get out.

"Beat it, you," he hollered. "Fucking *gadjo*!"

Walter got up slowly. "Hey, I'll leave," he said, "but don't threaten me or I'll take your head off."

Marie shoved him from behind and the man hit him in the face, then jumped back to where he'd been standing. Walter felt dumb. He wanted badly to leave but what could he do?

"I got a head like a rock," he warned the man, who seemed at a loss now that Walter hadn't gone for him or the door, either. He hissed. Was that a signal? Nothing happened. The man was just hissing. At him.

"'Gadjo,'" Walter spit back at him. "What the fuck's that? You some friggin' cat or something?" He moved to the door. "Hiss at me! Shit." He fumbled with the deadbolt but it wouldn't release.

The man moved quickly to open it, but when he tried to shove him out into the hallway Walter balked. The man drew back. He was taller, maybe six feet. He cocked his fist, then narrowed his eyes like he might hiss again. He thinks I'm a dog, Walter thought. He pushed the man clear across the room onto an overstuffed sofa. He got up with a knife.

Walter threw his left hand up as if to catch a baseball and the blade stuck firmly in the heel of his palm. But the man had lost his grip on the hilt. Walter grabbed his undershirt with one hand and ran him back into the sofa. He lay across the man's body with his head in a lock while he shook the blade from the heel of his palm. It clattered to the floor, a short thick Buck knife worth good money. The man was struggling harder. Walter threw it under the sofa and tightened his hold on the man's head. He felt strong. No one said anything. He looked up but Marie was gone. His fingers were sticky.

Then he saw the fat lady in the apartment doorway. She fell on him before he could offer to let the man up. Behind her, another man was jabbering in he didn't know what language. Talk sense! Get her off us, he wanted to tell him. She reeked of something. Laundry detergent? The second man grabbed both of Walter's legs and began to pull. He could hardly breathe. She had his hair with both hands, pushing his face deep into the lumpy sofa cusion. He swiveled his head for air. Now he was nose to nose with the man in his headlock. They inhaled each other's breaths. For one instant Walter thought of biting his nose, but he was getting air.

"Get her off me," the man sobbed. Walter inhaled the words without really hearing them. The expression "biting off your nose to spite your face" raced through his mind. He fought the urge to use what little breath he had left, and laugh.

"Let go," the fat lady said.

"My legs, let go." Walter could barely hear his own voice. His feet hit the floor.

"Let go now," she said.

Everyone let go. Somebody helped the fat lady up. Walter got to his feet. They were all there. Marie, an older man, the little girl. The man on the sofa, his face splotched with Walter's blood, began to hyperventilate. Walter remembered the door.

"Come back here and see what you did!" the fat lady yelled after him. But Walter was busy wrapping his hand in his handkerchief, and had seen all he wanted to in that face like a red boiled cabbage.

*   *   *

Walking to within sight of his front steps he heard an explosive pop. Short, sharp, but not a firecracker. A second shot popped and was buried in the sound of a bottle smashing. He was close enough now to hear Stevie Cole's voice.

"Plugged your litter bag," Tea Kearney said, pointing the muzzle of Stevie's .25 caliber automatic at the bag of empties behind Walter's thorn bushes. They'd been joined by an older man named Dekker who hung wallpaper for Myles. He was standing at the foot of the stairs watching Stevie tell a Vietnam story.

"Over there, you wouldn't believe it, them people, they're still drinking out of their hands," Stevie said, leaning out over his knees. Clusters of hair hung like horse blinders from either side of his head.

Walter stood with Myles by the open trunk of Dekker's car. He accepted a can of beer.

Kearney, looking sheepish, handed Dekker the gun. "Where you been?" he asked Walter.

"Out getting my palm read," Walter said.

Stevie had it now, small and flat and black in his upturned palm, and he was telling Myles how he'd personally forgotten more about weapons than any of them would ever know. "Myles, when I was in Army Ordnance you were still whacking off," he said.

Myles looked aside to Walter. "I didn't know you were supposed to outgrow that," he said.

"That's no lie either," Stevie said. He started to say something else but Walter had turned away and was concentrating on the paperhanging tools strewn around the beer cooler in Dekker's trunk.

"For example hand weapons," he heard Stevie say to Dekker. "Basically revolvers . . . automatic pistols . . . pin-fire, rim-fire . . ."

"And cease-fire," Kearney said.

". . . or central-fire . . ."

Walter, drifting with the rhythm of Stevie's words, remembered Beggar Harris. At Fort Hood, Texas, he had a line: "Wanna fuck, babe?" And the bigger the GI dance floor the better it seemed to work. "Arithmetic," Beggar would say. "Sooner or later it's all arithmetical," which he pronounced "arithmatickle."

Stevie was suddenly talked-out. Walter wondered if no one would move. A fine mist had adhered to his bare arms and face. Soon it would penetrate his clothes. And theirs. Still, no one moved. He could almost feel the deep black dye in his cotton jersey seep into his skin. The mist, the thought of the woman he'd never meet, the others' silence, all made him acutely aware of the time of his life and he put his hand out to Stevie for the gun.

"God*damn*, Walter," Kearney said. "What happened to your hand?"

"I fell," Walter said. Turning abruptly away from Stevie, he stood his unfinished beer on the roof of the car.

Halfway up the stairs he bent for a shell casing that lay against the soft wood riser. He rolled it in his palm. There'd been talk around of renovations. Who knew? He wondered if the same two black men would come back and fix his front steps. The others might all have been listening for the hollow ping as the spent shell hit the sidewalk.

"I'm going upstairs and wait," Walter said, chilled by the mist, for love, all the more convinced of it, for Amaris, for whomever God hath promised, for as long as it took. Yes. Already he felt better. There was no mistaking the tone of his voice. Much better. Now they could all come upstairs and wait.

SOMETHING TO TALK
LIKE A FAMILY ABOUT

Mrs. Sims paused, then punctuated her unfinished sentence by pursing her reedy lips so that her mouth disappeared.

"How's your philter?" Frank asked Mr. Davis, who put his empty glass back on the table. He lifted his cigarette delicately from the rubble in the ashtray beside the glass and pointed the unlit end at Frank.

"This look like it's got a filter on it?" he asked.

"'Philter,' I said. *Ph*-i-l-t-e-r. That's not a butt," Frank told him.

"Nor an 'and' or an 'if' either," a pleased Mr. Davis told Mrs. Sims, who was sitting between them at the short end of her kitchen table.

Mrs. Sims reached behind her head and coiled the loose ends of her gray hair back into a bun. Willowlike but hardy, she looked to Frank like the older sister of an elderly German aristocrat, an image he connected with her ten years full-time clerking in Langenscheidt's dimestore. Her salad days, he admitted. The last of the Langenscheidts, young Pfalzgraf who commuted, had readily agreed with Frank to pay half of Mrs. Sims's wages under the table, an expression she disliked. This arrangement, which she did like, gave her the full benefit of her Social Security check and more than enough mad money for bingo. Langenscheidt's was a small store, too, a neighborhood store where she never seemed to tire of the familiar faces or familiar items. It was only at the insistence of Mr. Davis, who was himself recently retired, that she'd quit her job three months before. Langenscheidt, of course, was miffed. "Misery loves com-

51

pany," Frank remembered telling her, his only objection at the time. Afterward, neighbors asked if he wasn't his mother's youngest and only living son.

But she was a bride again.

After a year's courtship and with Frank's reluctant consent, Mrs. Sims had recast her lot with Mr. F. A. Davis, their former milkman. Frank pictured in detail the brief ceremony, held in a corner office of the parish rectory, and the awkward walk home. Three months later they were still living among each other on the second floor of a very old seven-room beige three-decker in South Boston, just four blocks from an unswimmable fringe of the Atlantic.

"'Philter,'" said Mr. Davis, turning to Mrs. Sims. "Looked that one up near 'phony,' did he?"

Frank quietly ordered Mr. Davis to check the ullage between his head and his shoulders.

"Fry ice," Mr. Davis countered.

Instead, Frank watched his mother as she tried to collect the loose ends of the story she'd begun and lost earlier.

Mr. Davis was the first to speak. "Gathering wool," he whispered, eyeing Mrs. Sims sympathetically.

"Get it while you can," Frank told him.

To her friends and neighbors, Mrs. Sims had remained Mrs. Sims, or Brenda, and was not called by her new husband's surname. To Mr. Davis's further chagrin, every magazine delivered to the house, including Frank's *Ring* and his own Teamsters' newsletter, was addressed to "Ms." Sims. For this Mr. Davis openly blamed Frank, whom he characterized as a known postal worker with ready access to standard P. O. D. forms.

Mrs. Sims raised one hand from her lap and placed it flat on the table, both brace and gavel.

Soon she was remembering for them a pleasant incident, a story from her early school days whose relaxed telling appeared to mix warmly with the last few sips of her second whiskey and ginger ale.

"Beth it was. Beth something. A swell scout."

Mrs. Sims's long fingers ironed the folds of her rose housecoat, an early gift from Mr. Davis. She spoke carefully, as if she might be the only woman left on earth who still recalled the girl Beth.

"We were a quartet," she told them, her eyes fixed on the blackish cigarette pit that scarred the white and gold-flecked Formica top of her kitchen table. Frank sensed she was already deep in other thoughts, her mind tripped into reminiscence by the liquor or the sudden springlike weather that had thawed a very cold, snowless January.

"So you were a quartet," Mr. Davis reminded her. He lit another cigarette. Frank bridled.

Mr. Davis's chain smoking was something that at times so irritated him that Frank would secretly snuff out the butts where he found them, or if snuffed by Mr. Davis one remained smoldering in an ashtray, he would fill the ashtray with water, beer, ginger ale, milk, whatever was handy. With Frank off to work, Mr. Davis would get revenge by cascading the digits on Frank's new digimatic clock radio. Frank bore it all, for he saw in his new family situation a grand scheme on his mother's part to combat the loneliness that attended his own comings and goings. Only once did he tell her what he thought. "And if that's so," she'd said, "you've both of you only forced me into some kind of neutral corner, then."

Mr. Davis loudly snapped the lid over the flame from his sterling silver cigarette lighter—an early gift from Mrs. Sims—and placed it flat on the table. "Then what?" he asked, examining the inscription: BS to FAD.

"We were three," answered Frank, at thirty-five a muscular, balding man, tall like his mother, slim, he thought, because or in spite of the weekly workouts in his cellar weightroom. "A trio." His darker complexion he credited to an old family tale concerning relations between one of his Donegal forebears and a strong-swimming, unidentified Spanish soldier seeking high ground in 1588.

"No no, we were a quartet," Mrs. Sims repeated, "and Beth was at the end, she'd be the last one of us to go out." She stopped there.

"On stage?" prompted Frank, lately accustomed to his mother's sometimes disconnected reveries.

"On stage," she said. "In the auditorium behind the basilica . . . although it wasn't one then."

Frank: "A basilica or an aud—"

"That's right. We called ourselves The Sweet Tones." Mrs. Sims paused briefly between these last two words in order to make clear their separation. "The contest was open to everybody in the parish right up to the eighth grade, but all of us kids were only in the sixth then . . . all the kids except Ellen." She stopped again.

"You'll get back to Beth sometime before supper, wouldja?" asked Mr. Davis, who was running one hand over the cold humps on the kitchen radiator as he spoke, searching for a grip to support his backward-tilting bulk. In the other hand he gently rocked an empty glass.

"You making a trip?" Frank asked him, tipping the rim of his empty glass toward the pantry opening.

"Get off your duff," Mr. Davis answered.

Frank got up, his glass in his hand. "Go ahead, Ma," he said, removing his mother's empty glass from the table and placing it in the sink. "I can hear you in the pantry."

"It's not that much of a story," she admitted, and Mr. Davis said that she'd sure had him fooled.

"Well," she said, "we all had chewing gum in our mouths and didn't the nuns like that. *Are you chewing your cud, Miss Twoomey?*"

She laughed.

"But then someone called out, *The Sweet Tones*! Only it wasn't our turn yet because there was another group even before us—I remember it was a little boy with a jew's harp and Walter Donnelly with his ukulele, a duet." Mrs. Sims put both hands up to her cheeks as if to relive the shock. "You'll never believe what they called themselves," she told Mr. Davis, who just rocked his empty glass and looked at her.

Mrs. Sims: "The *Sour* Tones!"

"Wow," said Frank.

"Well, we had to go on anyway and of course we had no time backstage to put the chewing gum anywhere so, ha, Beth—she was at the end—she said I'll swallow your gum for you—she was really a swell scout—so we other three each gave Beth our wads and the next thing we were out on the stage in front of everyone's parents and the nuns and the priests and brothers from the rectory!" She laughed harder, forming pools as strange to Frank in those eyes as the sudden vision of the full whitewalls he'd once, drunk but inspired, painted on the front tires of a two-and-a-half ton army truck.

"What happened to Beth?" he asked, reflecting without regret on his summary court-martial.

"Oh," said Mrs. Sims, "we didn't need her anyway."

They all laughed then, and Frank said, "You were carrying her anyway, right?"

"Oh yes."

"So you was a trio anyway," said Mr. Davis, before looking indignantly across the table at Frank. "What'd you get up and not get me one too?"

"Get off your duff," Frank told him.

"I think Beth would've made a swell nun," Mrs. Sims said to herself. Moving very slowly, she took her husband's glass into the pantry.

"Less ice, Brenda," he said, and wondered aloud why were they all drinking together anyway.

Frank, with no ready answer, wondered about the same thing. His mother rarely drank more than a single highball, disliked beer, and associated wine with rumdumbs and cardiac patients, while he and Mr. Davis chose not to drink indoors at the same location. A ballpark would be all right.

"Too nice a day," Frank said, in such a way that his mother couldn't hear from the pantry, "to piss away in a gin mill."

When she appeared again Mrs. Sims was carrying two glasses and her lips were moving without making any sound. Keeping one glass to herself, she resumed her position at the narrow end of the small, rectangular kitchen table, son to her left flank, husband to the right. Frank stretched, watching her reedy lips purse, then invert, obscuring her mouth, which reappeared opening in the shape of his name.

"*Frank has got a vocation, Mrs. Sims.*"

"Right," said Frank, his T-shirt stretching with him, rising above the beltless loops of his rust-colored corduroys. It went with my Saint Jude's Progress Medal. Which I won for going from a fifty-one to an eighty-seven in eighth grade geography."

"*Oh sister*! That's the whole of what I could say. *Oh sister*. And you! *Does it mean I'll never hafta pay taxes*? The only thing you could think to ask."

"He was the patron saint of hopeless causes," Frank said, smiling in Mr. Davis's direction.

"Fourteen years old. *Does it mean I'll never hafta pay taxes*." Mrs. Sims appeared to consider the implication. Neither man spoke. "How I just wish sometimes you stayed in when you went away, Frank," she said.

"Right, Ma." Frank locked his hands behind his head, then laid them awkwardly on the table.

"That would've made me happy," she said. "That one thing."

With his right thumb Frank idly rubbed the miniature gold calendar attached to the watchband on his left wrist, his nail scraping at the tiny black numerals.

Mrs. Sims, looking preoccupied, mumbled something about the father of her four children, Frank Sr., whom she had to-day outlived by an even fourteen years. Frank imagined her thoughts forming in the peculiarly exact, clinical way she reserved for the dead or dying.

"What say?" said Frank.

"Nothing," she told him.

He watched her stare into the blackish cigarette pit that scarred the top of her kitchen table.

"All's quiet on the western front," said Mr. Davis.

"I can almost see his face," Mrs. Sims whispered.

"Whose?" Frank said. "Dad?"

"Baker's," she said.

Now, Frank too was staring into the tiny Formica pit, where for an instant he pictured the blank face of Dr. Abram Baker, stating at his mother's insistence the exact process of her husband's death. That she would know. Frank clearly remembered his own discomfort standing in a corner of the emergency ward while his mother stubbornly pressured young Dr. Baker to fill some great empty part of herself with words such as "myocardial infarction." Afterward the body was given a longer wake than is customary.

"Your father was accident prone," she said.

"Umm," said Frank, wondering if this information, wholly unrelated to his father's death, had in some way lessened her grief.

"Aaaah," said Mr. Davis.

"And then Patrick," she said, "with a . . . what?"

"Hemorrhage," Frank said.

"Subarachnoid hemorrhage," she said.

Mr. Davis lowered his head.

Frank remembered the time—1:35 A.M.—roughly forty-five minutes after last call. His older brother, Patrick, was killed crashing his car into a light pole on the Jamaicaway. The wake—to the further anguish of Patrick's wife—was at the insistence of his mother as overdrawn as his father's. Mrs. Sims was very sad but knew her son had been drunk. In time she allowed Frank to encourage her with the thought that Patrick had taken no one else with him. Patrick's wife afterward moved her two children from Boston, and was never heard from in the ten years since.

"Well, Brenda," said Mr. Davis, "one kiddo out of four. That's not bad now. Lookit in the war."

"You only have to give one in a war," she said. "Don't you, Frank?"

"Ah, one, one and a half," he told her.

"Bless you," said Mr. Davis, favoring him with a murderous look.

But Frank was thinking of his sisters. Of Rose, the firstborn, who lived with her third husband and four of her seven children in British Columbia, which for all practical purposes might have been at the end of the world. His mother blamed herself for Rose's apparent failures, and spoke regretfully of having worked either days or nights in the basement kitchens of a number of Boston hospitals for thirty years, or since Rose, just a girl, first entered school. And Rose was by all accounts a pretty girl. And Catherine, the baby of the family, who after many attempts finally left home for good at the age of twenty-seven. She was not recently heard from. Frank wondered if his younger sister hadn't found a peer group in the Merchant Marine. His mother continued to blame Catherine's remoteness all on her own old age, and only incidentally on what Mr. Davis often referred to as "these days."

"Still," she said, "that one thing would've made me happy, Frank." She stared up at the clock, the slack out of her voice. She'd drifted abruptly from a reverie Frank could only guess at, returning again to the one he knew.

"But I could see from the look on your face in the train that you wouldn't stay," she said.

"They wouldn't take as good a care of me as you do. I spotted that right off."

"I wouldn't be worrying about you now," she said. "I won't always be here."

"He will," Frank said. Mr. Davis stiffened.

"That's not at all funny, Frank." She glanced solicitously at Mr. Davis, who began to flex his lower jaw in an aggressive manner. "Can't we all be happy?"

"You not happy with the milkman here?"

"That's not a nice thing to say to him, Frank."

"What? Milkman?"

"You lummox," said Mr. Davis. "Bald-headed bag-a-shit."

"He's retired," she said. "And he's your father."

"That's not a nice thing to say to me," Frank told her. "And all I called you was a milkman," he said across the table.

"That ain't what you meant."

"Your *step*father," she said.

"Tell me what I meant. Milkman."

"You stiff. Goddamn *bag*handler."

"*Mail*handler," Mrs. Sims corrected.

"You're sitting awful close to that window. Pop."

"Fat lotta good that'll do you. Go back in your room, stiff."

Mrs. Sims sat back so straight in her chair then that the ice rattled in her glass, which remained wrapped in her hand on the table.

"Check the meat, Frank," she said. "Go do that."

"Sure, Ma." Frank began out of his chair. "What the hell?" he said. "We got nothing on, Ma."

"Oh," she said. "Well sit down then."

Frank sat down again as his stepfather in turn got up. Telling his wife to excuse him, Mr. Davis started toward the long hallway off the kitchen. He stopped in the doorway.

"Y'know Brenda," he said: "This kid here is all action. Like his pals around the Pub there. One night one of em's pissing and moaning about the way another guy's played his cards. 'I'm gonna rip you a new asshole,' he goes." He turned to Frank then, throwing his head back in a half-amused, half-commanding gesture. "What's his name there?"

"Hunk," said Frank, who remembered the years-old incident but was held now by the aura of superior knowledge Mr. Davis had begun to convey in the retelling of it.

"That's the one. Hunk. Well, while this Hunk was busy telling the other cluck what he wasn't gonna do to him, the switchblade he's carrying in his pocket—big as a sword, Brenda—it flips open and rips the lining right out of his jacket. And that's the end of it right there! Everyone laughing at him." As he said this he turned from Mrs. Sims to face Frank. "Well you might just as well've been laughing at yourself, baghandler, you and them others. Huh?"

"Could be," Frank conceded.

"*Huh?*" Mouth open, head cocked, Mr. Davis sucked his lower lip in over the remains of his bottom teeth. The gesture seemed to indicate that Mr. Davis knew when he'd one-upped a guy.

"But I think it was all done with mirrors," Frank told him.

"What a crockashit you are!" With that, he carried himself away on the thick soles of his plain black shoes.

Frank went into the pantry, thinking of the first time he'd noticed Mr. Davis. He remembered his attention being drawn to the end of the bar and the big man standing alone there sucking beer from the squat neck of a Pabst bottle. He noted the man's bib-style cord overalls. Immediately, Frank associated the overalls with some place or thing so familiar in one setting that it blurred the association in any other. He remembered thinking his friend Hunk might know. "An H. P. Hood milkman," Hunk had told him. "You're a wonder, Hunk," he'd said. "And do you know too if he parked his milkwagon outside? Did he leave it out front of the door?" "He don't," Hunk said: "He swings it around back." "Well, go and ask if he's run out of nipples, okay?" "Okay," Hunk said, "but write it down. Very easy for Hunk to forget what he don't understand." "For the *Pabst bottle*," Frank told him. "To go with his bib." "Write it down anyways," he could hear Hunk say, "and pin the thing t'ya lip Frankie." Frank caught his own lips moving then, and poured himself a double.

He came out of the pantry thinking about when he was a boy and his father took him to the American Legion Hall early one morning. At the bar he saw a graying, veiny man he nearly recognized. The man wore plain black shoes, black pants, and a soft-looking baggy white shirt. The shirt looked familiar, too, not like anybody's at home. "Father McParland's the Post chaplain"—smiling, his father had told him that. It took some years before Frank saw the humor. He was an altar boy then, he recalled, as if telling it all to someone else, and on top of that had never before questioned the military.

The mood that memory so evoked was enough to rekindle Frank's interest in himself. He was into the kitchen smiling remotely when the harsh, full, and familiar sound of unintelligible words— "*Bohzhe oopahsee! Nee oopahdee! Boodt ahstarōzhna!*"—caused him to look where he was going.

"Oh, tomatoes again, cucumbers," Mrs. Sims hollered back. "Watermelon, Sonya!"

He first saw the hem of her housecoat, then saw the rest of his mother leaning over the kitchen radiator and out the opened window above it. Mrs. Bazarov screamed, and her great waving arms threatened to ripple across the five feet of alleyspace between them.

"*Smahtri boodt ahstarōzhna nee oopahdee!*" she screamed, waving the massive arms as if to shoo a cat.

Frank was across the room quickly, jerking his mother back in and asking what was it she'd been doing out there.

"Talking," said Mrs. Sims, a little peevishly. "To Mrs. Bazarov."

"We talk tomorrow," Mrs. Bazarov told her. "You rest now. Tomorrow we talk. To bed now!" she bellowed, pointing at Mrs. Sims and indicating Frank was to execute her command. Then

the combination storm window shut and Mrs. Bazarov guardedly closed the half-curtains on her kitchen window.

"She says it'll snow, do you think it'll snow?"

"Where's the screen, Ma? What happened to the screen that
was here? Hey, Ma?" Frank poked carefully out the window.
The old, wood-framed screen, its black mesh turning to rust,
lay impaled on a broomstick in the alley below. The broomstick
in summer supported a tomato vine in the garden cooperative
of Mrs. Bazarov and his mother.

Frank pulled his head back into the kitchen. He blamed himself, ignoring as he had his mother's requests not to let the
storm windows sit another winter in the cellar. He would ask
Mr. Davis to assist.

The sound of the flush spread boldly down the hall, and Mr.
Davis strolled into the kitchen buckling the thin black belt on
his tan work pants. Into the pants he'd forced a lime-colored
Ban-Lon polo shirt buttoned to the neck. Mr. Davis:

"What was all that jibberish about? I could hear that blowzer
way back there."

"Huh?" said Frank.

"What was—Forget it! I said *allqueersaredeaf*."

"What?" asked his wife.

"Nothing."

"It was too long ago Ma, don't ask him, he's forgotten already."

"You'd be lucky to know everything I've forgot," Mr. Davis
said, "if that was all you knew."

"I'll return my encyclopedia," Frank said.

"Now what the hell kinda thing is that to be reading all the
time?"

"Well, how much do *you* know about aircraft carriers? Quick!
How many'd we lose by accident in the Second World War? You
were there. Tell me! Then tell me something, tell me anything at
all about Zoroaster . . . fat ass."

"Pardon your son's French, Brenda."

"You put on a good show, Pop."

"Yeh, and all the world's a stage, too," said Mr. Davis. "Now
you tell *me* who said that."

Frank was exultant. "Marcus Aurelius," he snapped.

"Get out your five-hundred dollar encyclopedia, my friend. Go back in your room there and get it out cause if I'm not mistaken *he* was 'Friends, Roman countrymen gimme your ears.'"

"Sorry. Pop. You're thinking of Patrick Henry."

Mr. Davis hedged. "And you'll wanna repaint that wall while you're back there too," he said.

"What wall's that?" Frank asked.

"'What wall's that?' You got more than one orange wall in there? That's what wall, you strange bastard. One of 'em Day-Glo orange and the other three federal gold he did them, Brenda. Christ Almighty! *Day*-Glo. Huh?"

"No no no no no," Frank said.

"No no," his mother echoed. "That's his . . . what?"

"Humble," Frank said.

"His 'humble' wall," she said.

"That's my humble wall," Frank said to him.

"Happy motoring," Mr. Davis answered, flourishing his drinkless hand at them. "T'ya both."

Now Mrs. Sims got up from her chair slowly, no longer third man in the ring, and started toward the hall doorway. Mr. Davis got up, too, with an eye to the pantry, but was forced to wait out impatiently his wife's careful passage in the other direction.

"Why in hell you always move so slow, Brenda?" he asked.

"I'd just like to stay alive," she answered, "long enough to make rhyme or reason of the seventy-six years I've spent on this earth."

She continued down the hall while Mr. Davis entered the pantry, and Frank said to neither of them that as a result of two months in the seminary he could to this day do the Hail Mary in Latin. It was his day off, and despite what he'd earlier said to Mr. Davis, he had pissed a good deal of it away in a gin mill.

In the lull Frank reached across the table and lifted a lit cigarette belonging to Mr. Davis. He fingered it thoughtfully, mindful of a boxer on the West Coast, a carpenter called The Windmill, who he was said to resemble strongly. Thinking about that resemblance he forgot where he was and snuffed the butt under his tan Hush Puppy. Chastised by Mr. Davis, who saw, he bent to pick it up, wondering how could he ever have done something like that.

"No consideration," said Mr. Davis, who Frank knew had really done his level best—that little—to combat his mother's loneliness.

Frank looked over at the smoldering heap in the ashtray and then flipped the butt into the sink.

"Get it outa there!" Mr. Davis told him. "Dumb cluck. Before your mother comes out and sees it!"

A little raggy by now, Frank thought he'd done the right thing, he said. His stepfather went to the sink and picked the soggy butt from the drain stop.

"I need your mother, Frank," he said. "She's a good woman. I been a bachelor all my life and she's all I got."

Another thunderous flush and Mrs. Sims, more herself, listed through the kitchen doorway.

"Get out the chops," she said to her son. "And a vegetable. What's that?"

"Nothing," said Mr. Davis. He threw the butt in with the trash and said he guessed that they'd all be swimming soon if the weather kept up, and didn't every Irishman in America love the ocean.

Mrs. Sims said that she herself wasn't much for it, "But oh," she said, "how my mother loved the water. Never went in. Just thought about it and loved it. God knows. My father now! Why was it always at the beach he'd be struck by the notion to go back across? We all knew he'd never. My mother would say, oh, she'd just tell him there's no jobs, Twoomey. That was enough. Then after supper I remember he'd go and groom Mr. Hanley's horses. I never could think of anyone but him as Irish though, and these others certainly aren't Irish to me." Mrs. Sims elevated her head as she spoke, indicating the rooftops beyond her two kitchen windows.

"Or my father, that thick, thick brogue too, he'd holler, he'd be, oh, half-mulled, 'There's not an Irishman *in* America! Only these,'" muting her voice as if for fear someone else might overhear the epithet, "'only these *g.d.* Americans.'"

"Well, he's gone now," said Mr. Davis with bowed head.

"And so will we all be one day," she answered.

"That's true enough," Frank agreed, laying lamb chops in a fry pan.

Then they were all silent.

"Did you know there's a bridge?" Frank asked, encouraged by their silence. "This is according to the Persian followers of Zoroaster, now."

It may have been the exotic name, or a sense of the malice toward him gone out of Frank's voice, but Mr. Davis lifted his head and appeared in fact to be listening.

"You have to cross over it after you die," Frank told them. "If you did the right thing it's wide enough and if you didn't it isn't and off you flip into hell."

"What's there on the other side of it, Frank?" Mrs. Sims wanted to know. Frank turned one of the chops.

"Didn't say a thing about that. *Chinvat*'s what it's, what the bridge is called."

"That must've been near 'Carriers.'" Mr. Davis's declaration was itself with malice.

"That's *A*," said Frank. "'American Literature' that was near."

"You said 'Chinvat.' *C*."

"That's right."

"In whose alphabet?"

"'Carriers' are *A*," said Mrs. Sims. "They carry airplanes. Let's not argue now we've finally got something we can talk like a family about."

"You were close enough," Frank told him, turning then to his mother. "Nothing to argue about."

"So anyway," Mr. Davis offered, "if there's nothing across it then there's probably nothing below it either and so there's nothing to worry about in the first case."

"That could be, too," said Mrs. Sims. "But what if you're in the least mistaken?"

"Hey, I'm with you anyways, Brenda."

"Then could you tell me, dear, where is it I'm taking you to?"

"I'll give you seven to three one or the other of you makes it," Frank told them, and said whichever one it was'll be sure to send back for him, wouldn't she.

Mr. Davis then said that it was a tough nut to crack, and in answer to Frank's latest, replied that he too preferred the mixed vegetables. Mrs. Sims, wife and mother, quickly agreed with the choice.

All were agreed.

"Don't tell me!" exclaimed Mrs. Sims, and they all laughed. "Frank," she said, "I think you should've gone on to school." She sounded in much better spirit.

"Oughta get himself married," Mr. Davis joyfully suggested. "That'll straighten him out, Brenda, huh?"

"Bennett Ashpy's none the worse for it, Frank," she said.

"Bennett's okay," Frank said, determined to stop her there, "and I've read where they say Thorstein Veblen did awright by the women. Then of course there's Humphrey Munga."

"*Softasasneakerfullashit*, that guy," Mr. Davis agreed.

Frank looked unsurprised at him, then turned to his mother. "Soo," he said. "How's Thursday then?"

"Oooooh," she said, and Mr. Davis spit the ice cube back in his glass to say that he'd give away the groom. Frank turned another chop.

"Want these things salted?" he asked.

"Oh, just a pinch maybe," Mrs. Sims said.

"How much in a pinch?" he asked.

"Don't be too smart now, just a smidgen I said."

"That's about a tad, right?"

"Do what your mother asked you fachrissakes!" Mr. Davis exploded. "You shitfaced or what?"

"All right, all right," she said. "You just be quiet. Go in the parlor now on the mantel and get my glasses, and I'll start the rice."

Mr. Davis left the room.

Mrs. Sims blotted her lower lids with a thorny knuckle.

"You're really all I've got," she said.

Frank turned his back to his mother and began to stir the

vegetables with added vigor, causing the timeworn pot to rock on its dents. He wrapped the thin metal pot handle in his fist.

"You're it, boy," she said.

Stunned at first by her cunning, Frank was another minute groping with the full sense of what she'd done. He continued to whip the foaming peas and beans and carrots and corn until finally he said that he wished for all his life that he had something, too. Mrs. Sims rose from the table, her right hand encased in a quilted mitt.

"You've got time," she said, more to herself than to him as he was already halfway down the hall cradling his palm. In the front room Mr. Davis hollered that the TV says it'll snow.

Frank, seated on the edge of his bed, saw him pass in the hallway. He could hear his mother in the kitchen say that he hadn't been very hungry, she guessed.

"No?"

"No," she said. "I think he's gone in his room."

"Yeh, he's back in his room now," Mr. Davis told her. "Watching those damn digits change on his new clock radio."

Frank lay back. Sunday he would check the classifieds, take a room if he had too, and not spend another week where he wasn't wanted.

THE MAN WHO WORE SUNLIGHT

One step ahead of his thoughts, John Shields strode out of the sun into the Boston Greyhound station. His bum foot throbbed. But he'd shined his worn loafers, thank Christ. You were only as bad off as you looked. He'd been to a shoe repair shop and had the left one stretched a full size to fit over his bandages. Sayonara, loafers.

He pressed on to the ticket window, his cane cutting the air like a swagger stick inches above the littered floor. Behind the window a woman sat forward on her stool, her long fingers kneading at her elbows and her shoulders hunched against the unnatural chill of the air-conditioning. If ever a woman needed sun . . .

"Do you need more time? Speak," she said.

"My turn, is it? Barnstable," he said.

She pulled her white angora sweater closer around her shoulders and went to work. He thought she only needed to be held. Some warmth. He could always fix her up with Manny. Now that Manny had a car.

"Think I'll go and lay in the sun for the day," he said. He smiled. She raised her eyebrows, which made her face look longer, as though he'd said something that should have embarrassed him.

He lowered his eyes to her hands as they made out his ticket. He was sure she was still watching him, ready to pounce at his next friendly word. What had put her off? The cane? His limp? He wasn't very tall—maybe on the short side—but even his wife said he was well built for thirty-six. And Carla, didn't she love his bristly red mustache? In his tan slacks and neat denim workshirt he looked, he thought, like any intelligent man injured while doing something athletic. His nose and the scalp beneath his thinning hair were pink from the deep burn that over the last week had faded from the rest of his body, but with a few hours in the sun . . .

He raised his eyes confidently but she was looking down at her hands as they made out his ticket. Did she care at all that he'd been shot?

What a week. Last Friday, while dining alone on Mexican food at an Irish bar and grill, he'd been hit in the foot by the ricochet from a .22 caliber target pistol. Another man had been the target, and the woman responsible, gun in hand, had apologized. "Dandy," Shields had told her, struggling to mask the pain. "Dandy, dandy, dandy."

At St. Elizabeth's Hospital, where he'd spent the night, his life had seemed to drift reassuringly out of his hands. He'd charged his treatment to the family medical plan his wife had taken out with her employer before she and Shields had separated. He'd advised the police not to press charges against the woman who'd shot him, not on his account. She did apologize, he told them. But there was a state law, and they had to. In the morning his medication wore off. He returned to his rented room, where he was kept up at night first by the throbbing in his foot and then by a lot of questions he didn't want to answer about the direction of his life. Before a week was out he'd said the hell with it. Today, Thursday, a perfect day in the middle of June, he'd packed an overnight bag and strode out of his room for the Greyhound station. And amen, he told himself.

He quietly paid for his ticket with the money that was left from the sale of his air-conditioned Chrysler. A major car. Worth more than the three hundred he'd got from Manny, the Filipino graduate student who had the room across the hall. A vision of the woman behind the ticket window, shivering in the front seat next to Manny, didn't make him feel any better about losing it.

Twelve-thirty; his bus was due at one. There was time to call

Carla. Or should he wait until he came back from the Cape? He
was nearly to the phone. Wait, hell. He'd had enough of that. In
the months after his marriage had broken up he had not had so
much as a date. Except for meals at the corner sub shop, or the
odd Sunday with his eight-year-old daughter, he hadn't strayed
far from his room. Then he met Carla at a Quincy Market
singles bar, where he'd gone on Manny's advice. She was on the
first stool by the bar entrance, a drink in either hand. He wasn't
able to move further in for the weekend mob. Her good looks
alone seemed to be keeping her from falling off her stool. He
remembered wondering if she was old enough to drink.

When they made eye contact he'd pointed in turn to each of
her drinks and said. "That one's a tequila sunrise and that one
could be almost anything."

She'd stared at the unnamed drink as if she hadn't known it
was there in her hand. "You're damn right," she said to him.
"Now give me one good reason to spend the night with you."

"Breakfast," Shields told her.

They spent the night in his room, and in the morning he'd
borrowed Manny's electric pot, some paper cups, and instant
coffee. "You-luck-out," said Manny gloomily, running the words
together in a way that made him wonder now if Manny, at MIT,
hadn't actually computed the odds.

He phoned Carla every day for two weeks after that, but only
got through to her once. She agreed to meet him for dinner. So
that she'd know that he knew his way around the city, he chose
an obscure Irish bar and grill specializing in Mexican food.
When she didn't show, he'd ordered the #4 El Phoenix Special
and, as was soon clear to him, been shot as much for that
choice as anything else. He'd been trying to reach her since. Finally he'd called the singles bar where they first met, and the
bartender had agreed to relay a message if it was no longer than
a name.

Shields studied the graffiti on the Greyhound wall, listening
to her phone ring.

"Carla?" he said.

"Carla's not here," a woman said. "Who's this, Schultz?"

"John Shields."

"Shields, Shields, right. Carla's not here, okay Shields? This is her sister."

"Tell her I called," he said quickly. Sister, my ass, he thought. But at the heart of Carla's beauty he'd glimpsed an erotic immaturity, and half her attraction now was in the unspoken challenge that, given the chance, he could not win her over again with some grand display of charm and wit. Something about the foot, maybe. She was out of work, unsettled, young of course, just off a soured affair, but who was he to hold anything in that litany against her?

As he hung up, he was drawn back to the graffiti on the wall. One piece he read over.

> I sat me down outside the ladies' restroom
>> in the Greyhound bus station
>> and vowed:
>>> If a woman with green hair
>>> and fingernails
>>> ever walked out, I'd marry her.
> She did and I did.
>> That's the luck of the Irish.

Signed, "Nick." Maybe there was something to be said for the Great Unloved. Their driven humor. He hesitated before phoning his wife—who he knew was not home—then went ahead with the call so that he would not be lying, exactly, when he maintained later that he certainly had tried to warn her he was coming. That done, he hobbled to the gift shop and bought a *Globe* with an eye first to listings under Professional Help, then General, and Business if the ride didn't put him to sleep.

The unnatural chill of the air-conditioning in the lobby drove him outside onto the platform by the bus docks, where he watched the slow traffic of people with purposeful looks and a tight grip on their baggage. Tomorrow, he promised himself, the beach.

The sun made purplish reflections in the oil puddles at his empty dock. His attention was drawn away by the warning beeper from the Vermont-bound coach backing slowly out of an adjacent dock. The only person near him was a teenager in tight jeans, her blouse quite open. She sat astride her suitcase with her back arced like a swimmer about to dive, a *Cosmopolitan* dangling at her fingertips. He knew he was staring. One of her small, pale breasts lay fully exposed in the fold of her blouse.

"Oh," she said. She stood abruptly. Shields smiled. Benignly, he hoped. "Oh," she said again, but this time it sounded so impenetrably sad that he knew it had nothing to do with him.

He turned to see a white-haired man in a gray suit trying to scramble from under the rear of the Vermont bus. Shields couldn't think of anything to say either, and for an instant he and the girl just watched the man scramble on his back. Then Shields took one wild step forward and hurled his cane at the windshield. It clattered off the glass and into a queue of people boarding the Haverhill Express. The girl ran out to the man on the ground. "You fucker," someone in the Haverhill queue yelled at Shields. But the man who'd been under the bus was on his feet now and Shields and the shaken Vermont driver had to convince him to lie back down and wait for an ambulance. Shields couldn't find any blood. The man's pure white hair looked like a clean bandage above his gray face. Shields took the driver's cap, put it under the man's head, then sent the girl for his own overnight bag and put that under the man's feet.

"I'm late," the man said, gesturing over his shoulder to the Haverhill Express. "Call my wife."

A crowd had formed. A nurse appeared, and the driver thanked Shields for his quick action. Shields thanked the girl for seeing the thing at all.

"I wouldn't like to be trying to get up to Vermont in a hurry," someone said.

Shields smiled uneasily. When the ambulance came he retrieved his bag, but all his bending had got the foot aching again and there was an oil smudge on the knee of his tan slacks. Yet he felt oddly at ease in spite of his pain, and in the face of what had just happened. Lightning would not strike John Shields personally, twice, no how. And if it did he'd be ready. Hadn't he already caught a slug ("One of life's better shots," he'd joked to the emergency room nurses at St. Elizabeth's) and walked away?

"Whew," said the girl who'd seen the accident.

"He'll be okay," Shields told her, though he was reluctant to believe it himself.

"I didn't know what to *do*," she said.

"You did okay," he said. Then he thought maybe he hadn't done all he could. It had happened in plain sight. Why hadn't he been more alert? "Heads up!" he imagined himself hollering.

"Did he call out?" he said.

"No. Unh-unh. It just, like *wham*, happened."

I didn't hear any wham, thought Shields. The girl appeared to consider what she'd heard.

"This place is gross," she said, looking around as though she'd just that moment seen it. They were quiet then.

"I'm going down to see my daughter," Shields told her. When she didn't answer he thought for a second she might know, somehow, that it wasn't his day to visit. "To the Cape," he said boldly.

"Me too." She smiled. "To the Cape!" she said, raising her fist in a cheer.

*   *   *

On the bus he was able to relax, with both seats to himself, although at the last minute before boarding there'd been crowd enough. All on banker's hours, he told himself. Off to the Cape to bliss-out in the sun. He'd lost track of the girl.

Half an hour later he was in *The Globe*'s Living section, disparaging the headline: "Love makes theories go round." He read the bold print above the copy. "In order to explain why we feel profoundly attracted to some people and why we can't stand others, theorists cite the principle of reinforcement: We like those who reward us and we dislike those who punish us." That made just enough sense so that he saw no point in going on. Sure he'd fallen behind in his payments to his wife, but how was that his fault? Thirty-six years old with a bachelor's degree in Speech. Why Speech? He tried to remember his undergraduate adviser's name. There'd been stranger lawsuits. As if to compensate for his lack of support, he'd started sending his wife sweepstakes and lottery tickets purchased in her name.

"As a *what*?" she'd said to him the first time he'd done it.

"As a sign of good faith," he'd said. "Jesus Christ, I'm hardcore unemployed right now."

"Right now?" He could still remember the tone of her voice. "You make it sound like you've actually worked in the last year," she'd said. They were standing with only the kitchen table between them but she could have been talking to a stranger on a long distance line.

The passenger in front of him reclined her seat. He recognized a patch of blouse, her *Cosmo*. She threw her hands in the air and stretched. He couldn't help thinking of her small breasts, the nipples taut against her blouse. He wondered what the poor bastard knocked under the bus might be thinking right now. Lucky to be alive. In bed with his wife, Shields hoped. If he'd been left with any sense. The girl tossed back the ends of her hair, smiling over her shoulder at him, then curled up so that all that seemed to be left of her was the luxurious clump of dark hair propped in the space between the seats.

Shields turned to a column headlined "The standards of beauty." He thought the columnist had good reason to wonder why Ava Gardner's name had been omitted from a new book on the subject. Jackie Onassis over Ava Gardner? What did "class" have to do with seeing a beautiful woman when she passed you on the street? He looked discreetly across the aisle for any sign from the woman there that his lips had been moving. Sometimes when he was upset . . .

They barreled south, across the Sagamore Bridge by the time he'd got to a review of a book about Carl Jung, "born on the Swiss shores of Lake Constance 109 years ago." He read on. "In 1903, the young Swiss psychiatric resident married a woman he'd fallen for when he saw her on a flight of stairs at 16, seven years before." Christ, for a pencil and paper. His mind worked quickly. "Dear Ms. White," he'd say, "I am an admirer of your columns. In the matter of Ava Gardner and Jackie Onassis. . . .

And if you see your book reviewer, no offense, but Carl Jung couldn't have been 16 in 1896 if he was born 109 years ago in 1875."

He woke as the bus turned into the Howard Johnson's parking lot in Barnstable. Shields waited politely half in and half out of his seat for a chance at the aisle. All on long weekends, he told himself. Summer hours. He'd like one of those jobs.

"*Ciao*," called the girl who'd been at the dock.

He turned, raising his cane hand to wave goodbye. Then stopped in midgesture as two things occurred to him. His cane was back at the Greyhound station, and his wife would not take his wound seriously without it.

"Sayonara, cane," he said. The girl, out of hearing, looked up brightly. Shields managed a smile.

He found a phone stand in the parking lot. But what would he say if Carla answered again and said it was her sister? How could he know it wasn't her sister? Know for sure. Or did it matter at all? He had to admit that it didn't, and then he was tempted not to call her. To his surprise she answered; he was still directing the operator to put the toll charge on his rooming-house phone in Boston.

"So what have you been doing with yourself?" Carla asked into that conversation.

"Me or the operator?" Shields asked, trying with his free hand to shoo the little terrier that had come off the hot asphalt. It lay panting in the shade beneath the phone stand, a blue bow in its hair and its muzzle on the toe of his bad foot. Shields looked around for its owner.

"What have *you* been doing with yourself?" Carla asked.

"Trying to get some sun," he said distractedly, "and picking fights with dogs."

"Again?"

"What do you mean 'again'?"

"Didn't you get shot or something?"

"I did," he said archly.

"I got there afterwards," she said, "and they were arresting this lady. I didn't know where they took you so I went to my friend's apartment who's near there. I don't know. He said don't get involved. You okay?"

"That's a friend," he said. "Say hello."

"I was in love with him. *C'est la vie*. No more of that shit."

"I talked to your sister," he said.

"My sister."

"This afternoon."

"Right!"

Shields watched the terrier, suddenly alert, scurry into the maze of parked cars. He quoted e.e. cummings from the Literary Calendar a previous tenant had hung in his room, on the subject of unlove ("the heavenless hell and the homeless home . . ."). She wanted to know if he wasn't scared, honestly, of being hurt by her inability to care about any man at the moment.

"If anything I'm frightened I'll catch one in the head next time," he argued. "Of course the answer to that is avoid Mexican food, or Irish bars. Whatever you can do to me is more in a natural order of things," he said, "and however much that hurts, it'll probably have been worth it."

Carla took a rain check on his offer of a midweek lunch date. "But call me anyways," she told him. So he would, that he would, he said, while on the great scale of things that could neither be weighed nor measured, he felt she owed him the call.

He phoned next for a cab, arriving at his wife's house in time to greet the sitter's school bus, get her house key, and dismiss her cavalierly ("With a two-dollar stipend for your trouble, my dear"). She was new to him and he caught her staring at the large oil stain on the knee of his slacks.

"Came back from the cleaners like that," he said. "Lawsuit there." She looked repeatedly over her shoulder as he watched her go.

Parting curtains and opening windows, he bobbed through the neat, airless rooms of the small Cape. Only his wife's bedroom seemed changed. (Or had he already forgotten the soft odors of a woman's bedroom?) He considered just signing over his half of the house to her. Settle up that way. From the day his wife had asked him to leave six months ago, he'd lived with the fear that he could quite easily become a deadbeat. Best to settle up beforehand.

Soon his daughter's bus would arrive. On the refrigerator

door the delicate crayon work of one of her art papers enclosed
a poem.

> Sunny, hot
> Swim all day
> Having lots of fun
> Today.
>   Gabriela M. Shields

She was so surprised to see him that she let the screen door
slam shut on her fistful of school papers.

"I'm making you a get-well card in school." She beamed at
him. He hoisted her in his arms. "My teacher made the whole
class write you one."

"'Made' them?"

"Mom told me about your accident. What kind of a dog was
it that bit you, dad?"

"A Lhasa Apso."

"So don't you even have a crutch?" she asked. "Where's your
car?"

Two of Gabriela's friends appeared at the door before she'd
had a chance to eat the peanut butter and lettuce sandwich he
fixed ("You can learn to live on these things," he'd assured her),
and she tore away.

"You should change out of your school clothes," he hollered
after her.

"I will," she hollered back.

The foot had begun to throb badly and he stepped out of his
loafers. He found his newspaper and burrowed into the den
couch, nearer than ever to the Help Wanted section. Or maybe
he'd try law school. Why else had he majored in Speech? He
could get a loan. Well, maybe he couldn't get a loan, but for
openers he could take his law boards. The idea suddenly coincided with his self-image as a late starter. Like the way he characterized himself at job interviews. He'd gone through the public schools in Boston, he'd say, then done this and that.

"There was the draft, a twelve-month tour in Japan, then a
bit of ennui, marriage, college on the GI Bill, my degree at
twenty-nine, some unchallenging manangement trainee posi-

tions, and, ah, three years in customer relations at Western
Electric."

"And you left that position for what reason, Mr. Shields?"
the last interviewer had asked as if he were sure Shields had
been canned.

"Of a long commute," Shields had told him. "The Cape to
Boston. I never got to see my daughter."

It still seemed like such a plain reason. Why couldn't he have
just said it was too costly? Gas, parking, wear and tear on the
old Chrysler. And found another word for *ennui*. The last one
("Thank you, Mr. District Attorney," Shields had said to him at
the end of the interview) had stopped short of calling him a
thirty-six-year-old beginner. Sayonara, job. His wife had gone
back to work little more than a year ago. Now she managed a
boutique selling "class" items, as she called them, for bed and
bath. She'd got a loan and bought into the business. A second
shop was in the works, she was driving a new Datsun and pull-
ing down more than he had in his best year at Western Electric.
He was suddenly filled with pride. If only she hadn't expected
him to do as well.

Gabriela reappeared then with a bouquet of ragweed and the
next-door neighbor's dog, Arnold, a big black and tan Rott-
weiler that Shields himself had named after seeing Arnold
Schwarzenegger on TV in *Pumping Iron*. So with the dog at his
feet and the ragweed in his fist, he saw little else to do but ac-
cept her offer that the three of them watch "General Hospital."
When the doorbell rang, Arnold lumbered after Gabriela.
Shields cocked an ear.

"Who was that?" he asked.

"Nobody," Gabriela said. She settled in again beside him on
the couch. Strange, the sense of privacy that stopped her from
saying more. Sometimes he worried about it. But best to wait
her out.

Last fall he'd stepped out to split a log, his wife was at work,
and Gabriela had answered the phone. Her taciturn manner—
she was her mother's daughter there, he was afraid—had cost
him a seasonal job pointing chimneys for a man he'd met in a
hardware store. "Just as well," he'd consoled her later, thinking

he was out of earshot of his wife. "You don't have an ounce of ambition left, do you?" his wife had said. There was as much discovery as anger in her voice. "*Voila*," he'd said. But back he'd gone to the want ads, mailing off resumes until it was clear to him that he'd need part-time work just to keep up with postal increases. Finally he'd interviewed for a middle-level job with a public relations firm. "Mr. District Attorney." Maybe he shouldn't have said it.

"It was only the babysitter," Gabriela said. "She just wanted to see if you were still here."

"I see," said Shields.

"It's only a Thursday," she said. "I never get to see you on Thursdays." Arnold looked up at him questioningly.

"I came down to visit you," he said. "But I'm really tired, too, since my foot got hurt, you can see it right here." He elevated the lightly bandaged foot as if it were secured with diver's weights. "So I thought I'd just rest some if it's all right with your mother when she gets home from work."

"I see," Gabriela said. Her face took on the emphatically murky look of real insight.

It was one thing to be too nearly understood by his wife—a woman he once loved, or did still, for all he could make of it—but quite another by an eight year old. "Do you?" he said. But she only pressed her lips hard against his, and he had to tickle under her arms to get his breath.

Later they played checkers over a faded sheet of cardboard with pieces made of Gabriela's old Tinker Toys.

"I remember when I made this thing," he said. "It was between the rounds of a fight I was watching on TV. See, I did these squares with a red Magic Marker."

"Weird," she said, taken up in winning.

When the phone rang she ran to answer. "Momma," she called to him excitedly. He steeled himself.

"The babysitter called me," his wife said, "and I just now got the chance to call you. What gives, John?"

"My foot—"

"I know," she said. "I'll be getting the bill, and that's as much as I want to know about your foot."

"You're covered."

"I pay the premiums, that's true."

"Christ," said Shields, "it's a good thing I beat the dinner check for my Mexican Special or you'd have to pick that up, too."

"You're very predictable, you know, John. The last time you descended on us like this you said it was to finish landscaping the yard. February. Wasn't it snowing?"

"Valentine's Day."

"How long before you can work again?"

"I'm thinking about law school now."

"*Law* school?"

"I suppose you won't pay for that, either?"

In the silence at the other end he could imagine the unsettled beauty of her smooth, broad, sun-darkened features. Seeing her picture in Shields's room, Manny had asked if she wasn't Oriental. "Half Italian," Shields had said, "and part Tabby on her mother's side." He grinned into the receiver. Where was her sense of humor?

When she spoke again it was in a monotone. "I don't love you," she said.

"Be that as it may," said Shields.

"What does that mean?"

He couldn't say. Half of him was still after the one good line to change everything. "My landlady's offered me some work," he said blankly. "When I'm better. Painting her roominghouse."

"Couldn't you substitute teach or something in Boston for the summer?"

"I've been shot once already."

She let out her breath slowly.

"They've laid off a thousand teachers in there," he said. "They're not going to hire me."

"I only wish for your sake you'd just get it together." Though the point of her call, she quickly added, was that she wouldn't be home till very late, for reasons of her own, and wanted to leave him with directions both as to supper and the one place he wasn't to sleep.

"And make sure Gabriela changes out of her good school clothes," she said.

"You really think I've forgotten that much already about being a father?" He put his hand over the mouth of the receiver and turned to Gabriela. "Go change your clothes, sweetheart," he said.

              *   *   *

Troubled by his inability to concentrate on the television, Shields was in bed in the den by eleven. He was up once in the night, caught in a dream that left him for a frightful instant, on waking, without a complete thought in his head. He shuffled back from the bathroom in the dark. Cricket noises replaced the sound of his wife breathing uneasily in their old bed. His bladder empty, foot blessedly numb, Shields again dropped off.

Toward dawn his dreaming was interrupted by the sensation of hot flesh at his back, or what he first mistook in a half-waking state to be his own overheated body. He struggled for his sense of place as one imperfectly formed image after another skimmed the edge of his consciousness. Because if he was still in his rented room, what godforsaken transient had crawled into his bed? But he wasn't there now, he determined sluggishly, feeling the den couch beneath him. Relieved to have gained his right mind, he reached back to acknowledge his daughter, as he'd done so often before, awakened in the old bed, and was astonished to find his wife.

"Consider this a one-night stand," she said.

It was over before he'd fully come to. He put his hands at her throat, then ran them over her smooth swimmer's shoulders to the tan lines on her breasts. She got up quickly and picked her robe off the floor.

"You'll sweat like that," he said.

She fastened the sash.

"You look good," he said.

She eyed him bluntly.

"I could probably lose a little more weight," he said.

"You'll never change," she told him, her eyes red now.

"Be that as it may," he said.

"Right." Her eyes began to clear. "And all this about law school?"

"Just a thought. Night school."

"Night school?"

"You're right. By the time I got through I'd be older than Carl Jung."

"Try thinking of someone else once, John. Of me. Of Gabriela. You're not being very responsible."

"Because I quit a thankless job—"

"No, John. A good job."

"—for what I thought were good reasons—"

"There was no reason."

"—and now I can't find another one?" He wanted to stand up and argue on his feet but he was naked. "That's not irresponsible," he bristled. "I have a very . . . adequate sense of responsibility."

"Dammit! You took me for granted."

"How could I love you if I could never relax enough to take you for granted?"

The anger went out of her smooth broad face. She seemed at a loss for the right words to describe what he saw was nevertheless still written there.

"I just don't love you anymore," she said.

"I know," he said quietly. "But you did once. What I guess bothers me so much now is that I never, ever really knew what you thought of me."

"I thought a lot of you. And now I think you're just enjoying yourself."

"'Enjoying myself'?" He looked down at his bandaged foot. "I can't tell you what a pleasure it is, standing up to flying lead, living in a rented room someplace that smells like the inside of a parakeet cage, foreigners in my car."

But the unaffected look in her eyes seemed to be telling him that he could; he was so thoroughly miffed that he couldn't form an answer.

"I'm sorry. I don't expect you to stay," she said, stalking away with all the force of a natural element.

He lay back on the couch. Sayonara, he thought. She'd even carried the pungent smell of their lovemaking away with her. Sayonara, Shields.

*   *   *

Breakfast went smoothly, Shields at the stove. Later he saw

them both off, with a kiss for Gabriela and for his wife a promise that Yes, he would clean up after himself and not run off with the morning paper.

With the dishes done, he felt better about napping. Then the beach, he figured, for sure by noon, well worth the trouble of a fifteen-minute walk, then back and gone as agreed. He hit the couch.

By noon he was up undoing the bandage on his foot, mindful of the healing power of salt water. He set off, in T-shirt, faded cutoffs, his flip-flops, and the morning paper. The neighbor's dog, Arnold, fell in, circling back constantly as if to be sure Shields really meant to go somewhere. Shields paused several times to peer down at his instep, taking readings on the condition of the round, thin layer of scar tissue over his wound.

At the beach Arnold raced after sandpipers, skirting the few blankets where women sunned with their toddlers. Shields walked to a shadeless expanse of low, uninterrupted sand dune. He removed his T-shirt before opening his paper to the heat of the day. First things first, he told himself, studying the headline on page one. He alternately read, bathed the foot, or simply rested with the T-shirt under his back and the paper under his legs against the hot sand. Once, over the top of the sports page, he caught sight of a string of lobster buoys, bobbing with each swell like the heads of so many white-haired men. The thought of them that way made an anxious lump in his stomach.

He put the paper aside. If he had to, could he swim out to them, he wondered, with his foot as it was. He half-wanted to hear someone call Help so he could drown trying. What would his wife say then about "just enjoying" himself? Shields contemplated the specks of white out on the swells. He thought of the people he loved. And for a moment or two, he loved them all. Gabriela, his wife, Carla, the girl at the Greyhound dock, even the woman in the ticket window. What was it of cummings on his roominghouse calendar, "lovers alone wear sunlight"?

He felt lightheaded. Though he was in no hurry to leave, he put on his T-shirt. The resistance of the pink flesh at the tops of his arms said burn. The dog was gone. He tried to estimate by the position of the sun how long he'd been out there, but one look down at his foot told him that. A wonder he hadn't felt it!

One step ahead of the pain, Shields took up his morning paper and covered the melting scar tissue on his instep. But what good was that now, and how far could he walk with his foot in a newspaper? "Sayonara," he said, and kicked it away. There'd be no relief. He watched it tumble in the breeze. Sayonara? That wasn't even his paper. He hopped after it on the good foot, trying to keep the sand out of his wound.

THE TERRIBLE SPEED OF MERCY

Padraic fixed the peak of his red and blue baseball cap, steering his boy down the sunless ramp from the ballpark to the street. The cap was a keepsake from another Red Sox pennant race, the joyful upset the papers had called an "impossible dream." Today he'd worn it for the boy. He'd meant a tender joke, simple monkey-faces. But it was like raising your voice in order to be understood by foreigners, he decided, this business of treating a full-grown man with a mental problem, your own son, as if he were a child again. God have mercy, he suddenly wanted to say, but Padraic thought He never did.

It was no one's fault. He was sure of that now. The boy was tragic. After an outstanding season of triple-A ball with Paw-tucket they'd brought him up to the majors and at the age of twenty he'd won as many games and broken a league record for shutouts. He was a giant of a boy, handsome as his deeds; born and raised in the same sports-crazy town he'd brought to within one game of the pennant after moving back in with his mom and dad. A sensation, Padraic reflected. The "Hometown Phe-nom," the sportscasters dubbed him. In the off season he took a minute to play catch with his kid brother and threw out the arm. It was as simple as that. At his agent's urging he held out the following year for a staggering contract. Word spread of the arm. To quell the rumors he appeared for spring training, where he set an informal record for wild pitches. Sent down unsigned, he had a fit, literally, and when Padraic came to get him he was already catatonic.

Jostled, hungry now, Padraic reset his cap against the cold

September wind. He tried the neck of his benchwarmer's wind-breaker, though it was zipped tight. At medium height he was underweight, if muscular for a man of forty-five, and his slick-ered, graying hair and long, carefully trimmed sideburns gave his nose a razorlike prominence. They were a pair, he thought. Him with the look of a man hurrying to a warmer climate, while the boy at his side might have been basking in the heavenly spotlight of his one good season.

Taking his son gently by the elbow, he said, "A nice street, I used to think. Seedy now." Souvenir stands, fast-food shops, the bars. Padraic doubted even the fine grounds crew at Fenway could do much with that landscape.

"Though it's about like always," he said, carried along as much by the crosscurrent of odors as by the flow of the crowd. Exhaust fumes, food frying, tobacco and perfume and beer. He took them in with his nose in the air and his eyes on two women chattering in Spanish. Barely his son's age. He was aroused by the rhythm of their gestures. Or was it just the look of them in their blue jeans, which might have been shrink-wrapped over their behinds by a picture framer? Padraic began talking quietly to the boy as if he understood.

"Know how you go away, then come back after a long while and everything's smaller looking? The buildings, streets you've always known. Well this street here got, by God, bigger. Since a year ago, was it?" His voice fell and he finished the thought to himself. "The simple fact is the ballpark there is the only thing that's looking shrunken," he'd wanted to tell the boy. But here he was absorbed again in his own thoughts, when the point of their outing was therapeutic, and had little to do with his deep sense of waste at not using their more or less permanent box seats at least once in the season.

His son, however, remained mute, gawking in slow, labored movements at nothing. Padraic was aware that children and adults alike were staring up in awe at the boy, half his own magnificent creation.

"Catch the Yankees is the only thing. We got the pennant, you think?" a man Padraic's age fired up at the boy.

"Right," Padraic hollered back, "the only thing now!"

The man pressed closer, several young boys on his heels waving Red Sox yearbooks. "Can he sign a thing?" the man shouted into the wind.

"What?" yelled Padraic. But when he saw the lineup card in the fellow's outstretched hand he shook his head vigorously. The man drifted away. The crowd thinned. At the next bus shelter the boys gave up.

Yet it was no one's fault. He was sure of that now. Pressure was to blame. Pure and simple, like some holy force, it stood as sole author of his son's misfortune. Total care, the doctors had told him, dark and wordy in their long shrouds. Months passed, and the boy underwent what Padraic learned to call a "qualified improvement." Now the family took him weekends, by the hand, smiling painfully for him through the simplest functions, studying his vacant expressions, and learning to talk as if he didn't exist.

But every cloud has a silver lining, Padraic could to this day picture his wife telling him in bed, fatal and innocent. Hadn't he himself got a good job out of it? And she was right, too, he knew it, to take heart at something, even at the left-handed generosity of some local politician, a baseball buff. The dirty bugger had later leaked it all to the papers, how he'd gotten this sad kid's dad a secure job for the first time in his life, collecting tolls from a booth on the turnpike. In a shit-colored uniform that made him itch, he might have added.

Though in one sense it was better now—both for him and the wife—than before the boy's big season. He'd been a roofer too long, out there with younger men who wore tattoos and called him "Irish." He'd had enough of it, enough of them, enough of hard work and merciless weather, of slow, drunken nights that always became morning just as he'd put his head on the kitchen table. Nor was it steady work, he reminded himself. And while the ball club had readily agreed to cover the boy's ongoing medical expenses, on top of the gift of two more or less permanent box seats, there were five younger kids plus his wife to support.

On the other hand there were times, like now, when Padraic imagined that anonymous plea on his own behalf. "Help the guy out," it went, "got a kid used to be a star's soft-as-a-grape now."

If nobody really talked that way, they might just as well have. Padraic began to wonder solemnly about the shapeless, bitter thing that these days muddled his thinking, and was astonished to hear himself ordering a double. He made eye contact with a surly bartender. (How had he come in there? And could he afford it?) Then his guts sank. Where'd the boy gone?

"A screwdriver, double, and what's he having?" the bartender wanted to know.

"My son?" he said, as if he hadn't come in with him. He looked up and saw the boy pressed in by his side at the bar. He immediately relaxed and order him a Coke. To avoid embarrassment, Padraic took a stool.

When they'd been served he reached out stiffly and peeked at the tab, as if examining the cost of their drinks at arm's length meant he might not have to pay the whole thing. Acclimatize yourself, he thought, while the bartender kept staring from his baseball cap to the boy standing stock still and perfectly erect at his elbow. Who was *he* to stare, with his hair in a woolly permanent and a tiny gold spoon hung from his neck on a girl's thin chain? He wanted to tell the pear-shaped bastard he was just a bit past it himself, too, to be wearing one of those skintight, college-kid T-shirts. Or was it a bicycle ad? COLUMBIA was all it said across it. Padraic removed the cap and folded it into his coat pocket. Processions of concessions, he told himself, watching the bartender stroll away without comment.

So this was a singles bar. His contempt for the man grew. But didn't this same spot used to be little more than a corner tavern? He placed it now from years past, a cheap after-the-game stop for sports talk. He wondered if they talked sports here anymore, or was it all sex? No matter. He decided not to stay around long enough to find out, what with youth and looks nowadays the timely thing, and that place and everyone in it right up to date.

Examining the crowd he was surprised to find his attitude mellow. The music took him home. The Bee-Gees, Donna Summer—birthday gifts the wife had got for him to give to one or the other of his children. There was a fellow playing the records and exercising his neck in an alcove off the bar, though it was early yet for dancing. He absently ordered up another for himself and then reached over and fit the untouched glass of Coke in his son's fist, encouraging him, with a smile and a brief charade, to drink.

He unzipped his windbreaker. For the first time that day Padraic looked purposely at his son. He had to hide his surprise at seeing the boy outfitted as he was, with the stylishly flared dress jacket and half-open shirt (silk, was it?) exposing his chestful of downy blond ringlets in a broad *V*. His mother's doing, no doubt, but here he might have been one of them. She'd be pleased finally to be fooling someone. Surely the night nurse was never fooled when Padraic returned on Sundays with the boy, his duds passing for the good life.

He watched the boy's jaw slacken further to accommodate the glass, but the sound of him slurping Coke became such a roar in Padraic's ears that he turned away. For in truth he'd always feared his oldest son had little else to market but a good arm and an eyeful to the lookers. The boy had been a remarkable athlete, as Padraic hoped he might once again be, but his looks now seemed a major part of that, too. Hadn't the family been forced to take the home phone out of the listings for all the strange women calling that one year? The boy would sit at attention, the receiver to his ear, as if weighing each outrageous proposition. After an hour or more, the caller would hang up. Still, the joke went around that with another good season he'd make more in lingerie commercials than Namath. It was all timing, like they say. Which left his younger kids struggling with half their brother's looks, no fastball, little more sense, and Padraic himself at the mercy of his love for them all. How in God's name did any of it really happen, he wondered.

Here he was, overcome again by melancholy. Lately this was chronic, and seemed to grow more in proportion to the glitter of a place than to how much he drank there. The bigger the realization of his own disappointments, he supposed, out among smartly dressed spenders. Anointments of disappointments. He was not altogether sure if the greatest of these wasn't his one lost chance to sit back comfortably for the rest of his life, on his son's laurels. Padraic raised his glass and silently offered the toast that in any event his was one boy saved from the bitter letdowns of a longer life in his right mind.

"Cheers," a woman said. To him? He turned and saw her on the stool at his son's other side. It was the boy she was toasting, whose vacant look down at her might have been mistaken for aloofness. She saw Padraic.

"Together?" she asked, leaning out over the packed bar so that her behind made a lovely heart tight against the fabric of her ivory jumpsuit.

"My son," he said. "Cheers."

The boy keyed in on their motion, appearing to join in the toast as the three of them in turn drained their glasses.

"Think I recognize him!" she shouted over the next record, shortening up on her sentences like someone unwilling to be drunk. "Am I ugly or why won't he talk to me?"

"Neither thing," Padraic shouted back. "He had an accident."

She came off her stool and stood between them. "Like what kind of an accident?" she asked, bluntly eyeing the boy.

"Lots of pressure." He pointed to his own temple. "He's a little distant now."

"Ooyyy," she said.

"He'll be okay later," he heard himself say.

"How much later?"

"I honestly don't know," he said in a lower voice. "But he's coming along."

She leaned in confidentially. As Padraic cocked his ear closer to her lips she hollered over his head to the bartender for another Galliano stinger.

"Oh I'll get that," he said, straightening up. He ordered again for himself and the boy, but when the drinks came she ordered them put on her tab.

"Hey, I work," he said.

"Who doesn't?" she said.

There was an awkward silence as both considered the boy.

"I knew I recognized him, probably from TV, and my youngest brother still trades baseball cards for that matter," she said.

"Only I forgot all about his accident and he wouldn't say anything back, so I kind of figured, you know . . ." Her eyes di-
rected him to two young men seated by the pinball machine,
diagonally across from them at the end of the L-shaped bar. "I
mean he *was* looking."

One of the men was staring openly at the boy, who, Padraic
noted, was indeed looking in that direction. The bozo eyeing
his son had thick yellow hair hacked up over his ears like a
woman with a boy's cut. The sleeves of his pullover were draped
over his shoulders and wound in a loose knot. The other wore a
see-through shirt and might have been the blond's brother if
they weren't holding hands now in plain view.

"It's the pinballs ringing he sees over there," he snapped at
her. "It just attracts his attention, that's all."

"Fine by me," she said. "Can I still talk to him?"

"He won't really understand."

"We'll see," she said as if Padraic had the problem.

Let her tinker, he thought, she couldn't do any worse than
the doctors who never bothered with him now he was off the
sports pages. At any rate he was back among his own. Kids,
sure, but they took an interest. Padraic could hear the names of
young, single ballplayers flying thick and fast at the boy, and did
he know this one and that one. Another woman had joined the
shapely one in the ivory jumpsuit, using wild hand signals in
her own effort to rouse him. So far between them they'd only
managed to wrap another Coke in his enormous mitt. Though in
time they also engineered a goofy half smile, the first in a year
out of the boy. Who was taking it well. Padraic wondered if their
attention might not be just the therapy for him. He watched pas-
sively as the second woman caressed the fingers that knew some
half a dozen change-ups. The two homosexuals looked on, and
each time the pinball machine rang up a big score the boy's
head rotated in their direction, but his eyes looked through
them.

After listening in on the two women at work, the same surly
bartender approached Padraic.

"Are you really his dad?" he asked. Soon he was telling how
he'd followed the boy's shortened career closely, even seen him

pitch his twentieth win, but just didn't happen to recognize players out of uniform, "although you will see them in here. My error," he said.

"We'll take that up with the official scorer later," said Padraic.

They laughed comfortably, with Padraic accepting on his son's behalf the offer of a screwdriver and another Coke.

"So what's his mother like?" the woman in the jumpsuit was asking the next minute.

"Dusts and cleans a lot," he said, "but I help around the house, too."

"Dusts and cleans a lot." When his face didn't change she said, "It was just rhetorical, you know, a *rhetorical* question."

"'Rhetorical.'" He might have been spelling it. "Did you want to know what she looks like?"

"Unh-unh," she said, shaking her head so that the dark waves of her hair caught the track light overhead.

"Well, she's in great shape."

"Good for her," she said. "She must work at it."

"Just the lower part of her face is a little pinched. Account of age. Still, you put her in a surgeon's mask," he said, "you'd have a great thing to love there."

"That's not nice," she told him.

How much better than her he knew that. And yet for the distance his wife had put between them in recent years, he thought she might just as well be wearing a mask. Or it was him in it.

He listened to himself making the best he could of that damp confession. "Like you see a lot of those people in Japan wear on TV," he said. "On the news about demonstrations and such over there. Or a veil like the Arabs do."

"Still not very nice."

"I can be nice," he assured her. He glanced over to check on the boy. The woman at his side placed a comforting palm on his forearm. The warmth of it there seemed to burn through the nylon sleeve of his jacket.

"He's in good hands," she reassured him.

"I hope so," he said, seeing his son mechanically raise another glass of Coke to the great satisfaction of a small crowd. There was the bartender, the two homosexuals, the woman who'd been holding the boy's hand. In fact, the boy had quietly been shifted down three stools to accommodate some additional onlookers.

"Because I have to go to the men's room," Padraic said.

She pointed out the woman at his son's side. "Don't worry," she said, "she used to live with one of the utility infielders."

"Ah!"

"I've forgotten, what's-his-name-there or someone."

"Right."

"Fryar, Edelstein? One or the other."

"And Hagerty, yeh. I know 'em." It wasn't so much of a lie, since his son had once introduced him to the entire team in the postgame din of the locker room.

"Do you really?" she asked. "How about Gibson, that one the players call, ah? . . ."

"'Hoot,' isn't it?" He rose smoothly. "I'll be back," he promised.

She took his stool. "Go," she said, hollering after him, "I'll hold this!"

In the men's room he shed his windbreaker and waited for a free urinal. He was all too aware of the younger men there, eyeing them two deep at the long mirror over the row of sinks, warily at first, as they angled like fashion photographers for the right position to restyle their hair with their picks and combs, their fingers, or painstakingly probed their eyes (for signs of what? he asked himself), and sprayed their mouths and noses with tiny atomizers. He'd never feel vain again for the few minutes he took to shape his sideburns on the days he shaved. He was truly put off, stepping up to relieve himself. These weren't even the gays. Younger men, sure, but looking around, Padraic thought he could kick ass if he had to.

He stepped away with a fresh cockiness and his jacket tight in his fist. When he saw the vending machine in the side wall he took his own sweet time before choosing a cologne. English Leather, lime scent, a dime a squirt. He set out, but not before he'd undone all four buttons on his polo jersey and exposed his undershirt. The fellow behind him walked up on his heel. Padraic spun, waiting in place for an apology.

"Excuse me," the young man said. His face was too straight. "You okay?"

Answering "Yes," quickly, Padraic continued out to the bar. She'd kept his stool. "Back so soon?" she said.

"Lotta guys at the mirror," he said. "Had to wait in line just to shave, never mind the shower."

"I've been in and out and everything already."

"Keep it," he insisted as she tried to give over his stool.

She nodded in the direction of the men's room. "What do you guys really do that takes so long in there?"

"Oh, things." He noticed his son still had his contingent. The woman at his side appeared to be exercising his fingers now. Or no, he saw what she was actually doing was—

"Signing autographs," his own companion informed him. "She helps him move the pencil. The letters come out pretty big, but what the hell, lots of people wanted them anyway."

"Yeh?"

"Sure. Just because he's sick people don't, you know, forget like overnight."

The bartender set them both up again and walked back to the register to ring it in on someone else's tab. Padraic hollered "Thank you!" into the crowd, and remarked to his companion on the plain human comfort in that place.

"Call me Nancy," she said.

"I'm Pete. People call me that."

"Why shouldn't they?"

"It's the name of the saint I took at my confirmation in the old country. I use it," he very carefully explained, "which is because my wife is what you over here call 'Irish,' her parents are 'Irish,' her friends are 'Irish,' my neighbors are 'Irish,' and no one can say, *Por-rick*."

"Which is what?"

"My name," he said. "But call me Pete."

"'Pete.' Like *for Pete's sake*?"

"Right. And *peat* the fuel. I've fueled a few fires in my time, too."

"I'll bet you have."

"I'm forty-five years of age but I've been a roofer most of my life and that's tough work, and you better know it." He was startled to find himself sounding like the men he humored in gin mills. And here he was out in the field as it were.

"You're in super shape," she said. "Can you jog?"

"Don't have to," he boasted, wondering in the same breath if she thought for some physical reason he couldn't. He gripped the edge of the bar tightly with one hand, making the already stark cords of muscle appear to separate from the bone down the length of his stringy arm.

"And that goddamn toll booth isn't about to soften muscle one, either," he added in the event she hadn't seen.

"What toll booth?" she asked.

"Nothing. How old are you?"

"Twenty-three."

"Old enough."

"For what?"

"Whatever you want."

She took his hands in hers. "We'll see," she smiled, back in command for several more minutes, or until he promised that he'd take her out to a special party soon, where she would meet the ballplayers. Fryar, Edelstein, Hagerty, the lot of them, even the mysterious Gibson. She was elated. He found himself with another double.

He thought eerily of the time he was having. What with Nancy at his elbow confiding in him about her consciousness, her personal habits and the kind of men that aroused her. This was new.

The bartender rejoined them. "Seems a lot more relaxed since he sat down," he reported. All three looked to the seated boy. "Keep him coming in like this he'll be cured before you know it."

"Honestly," Nancy chided him.

The bartender's smile vanished. "I meant like in with *people*, or out with people—"

"Up the people!" said Padraic.

"As a sort of peer group therapy," the bartender continued, "if that's warranted by his progress here tonight, and his own physician agrees to that." He took his case then to the father directly. "But bring him back in again next Sunday anyway, okay, the owners won't mind. Hell, they'll love him."

Padraic, anxious to experience the prettiest lay of his life, very nearly found himself agreeing to do just that. Half his age, too, and no roommates she'd said. He blamed his seven or eight doubles for the missing half of his erection as Nancy slipped her fingers under his waistband and drew him close in against her leg. Though she was clearly half in the bag herself. He promised himself he'd be more careful of that for the both of them when they met for real. For now he simply ran his hand along the inside of her thigh. She smiled. He broke into a short chorus of "Don't You Feel My Leg, Don't You Make Me High" (". . . cause if you feel my leg, you're gonna feel my thigh, and if you feel my thigh . . ." he crooned).

The bartender shot past him waving a large white rag. Nancy removed her hand from his waistband.

"What's the matter?" he asked.

"You'll need my number," she said. "Hand me my bag?"

It was at the foot of her stool. He bent for it. Nearby he heard the bartender asking for the second time across the bar if anybody had spilled anything or not. He freed her bag from between the forward legs of the stool, but its long shoulder strap caught on one of her platform heels. The shoe dropped. Padraic bent down and replaced it with a flourish as again he overheard the bartender, this time asking loudly if there hadn't been a drink spilled why had one of the young ladies sent him for something to mop up with?

Straightening, Padraic placed the bag in her lap. But she was looking past him, and merely raised one hand from her side to prevent it falling back to the floor.

"Nancy?" he said. Their eyes met. Then she craned her neck again for a better look at what was behind him. A queer look, he thought. He followed her gaze.

The group around his son had spread thin, he saw, and the stool on either side of him was vacant. The boy sat up straight in his seat. People passing near there circled gingerly in a wide arc. The bartender came around with a mop and a hard look for Padraic, who lowered his eyes to take in the dark stain etched over the boy's tan pants. He went to him, ignoring the bartender's warning to lift his foot, and watch he didn't go tracking the stuff. He felt the mop slosh over his shoe.

"Incredible," said the bartender. "Where to Christ was he keeping it, in a reserve tank?"

Nancy appeared to open her mouth to speak. Padraic thought she wasn't to blame. He was just as relieved to see she'd put her bag back under her feet. He realized how hungry he was; that the boy hadn't eaten either since his mother gave him lunch at noon; that he'd have to find the car; that it was Sunday, and what he'd done; that in the morning he'd be to work, encased in the small glass booth from where he watched the world go by.

They stopped once on the way out, at the end of the bar, while Padraic drew the red and blue baseball cap like a revolver from his jacket pocket and fixed it squarely over his ears. He took his son by the elbow, and the two made their way to the door in silence. In fact to Padraic the only clear sound now was the squish of their wet soles on the polished floor. God have mercy, he badly wanted to say, but then caught himself wondering if it was really necessary to ask.

THE MAN WHO SAVED HIMSELF

Dennis Stuart was an older boy. When he wasn't killing pigeons with his slingshot, he was fighting like a banshee with the first one of us he could corner. He lived in a brick apartment house with a copper bowfront, since razed, a short block from my old flat in Boston. We finally calculated the risk, three of his worst victims, and lay for him in back of Hanley's stables one day after school. Together we beat him for near a half-hour. We'd had to. He wouldn't stay down. Mr. Hanley, who hired out carriages (my father groomed the horses), told everyone that from what he'd seen the boy seemed to enjoy his beating. But my father never said a word to me about it, and soon afterward the Stuarts moved away.

I don't know if their move was connected to the beating. Years later I heard a story from one of the other boys involved, whom I met unexpectedly on a trolleycar. Dennis Stuart would have been in his midtwenties by then. My friend had pried the story from Dennis's older brother, who for one reason or another had come back to drink and play whist in the tavern where Hanley's stables had been. I learned that Dennis had fought some men in a barroom in another neighborhood, and not surprisingly was the only one arrested. He'd hanged himself in his cell the same night. His brother, after revealing that, had seemed embarrassed. Embarrassed, my friend thought, because Dennis, even in his desperation, hadn't held out for at least one more beating.

Now that's a true story, for what it's worth, and just one example of the things that have been running through my mind. They keep their own schedule.

I'm eighty-five. I had a stroke and wound up here. By the time I recovered I'd decided to stay. "Next time you'll lose your power of attorney," I told myself, "not just your faculties. There's no telling where someone will put you."

My room overlooks a herring run on the edge of the grounds. In spring you can hear the children who flock to see the small fish struggle upstream to spawn. The main house, a seventeen-room Greek revival, was built in the last century by a gentleman farmer. Someone added a rear deck, someone else a solarium. As an architect I know a good house. This one is thirty-five miles south of Boston on the way to the Cape. It's owned corporately, you never see who gets your check. They've been getting mine since January 20, 1974.

Mrs. Apps, the young evening nurse, tells me she can make out a bend of the North River from my window. She says the family of a previous owner, a dentist, left behind many of the Victorian furnishings. The current administrator complemented these with items from the Sunday flea market at the Neponset Drive-In Theater. In the activities room there's an old Capehart TV with a thirteen-inch black-and-white screen in a console the size of a small refrigerator. My eyes are shot anyway. The last thing I ever saw clearly on it was a movie, *The Sundowners*. It ran through several commercials before our Millie realized it wasn't one of her soaps and switched channels.

But in the study there's a grand piano and a shelf of Charles Dickens's complete works. Downstairs Mr. Fitzpatrick, a well-known spiritualist in his time, has undertaken to complete *The Mystery of Edwin Drood* by automatic writing. He insists that I act as his editor, sending via Mrs. Apps each infrequent page as he completes it. She corrects his spelling, and in his case I think she's right when she says that what he doesn't know won't ever haunt him.

The study is a quiet room with French doors and a window seat. I'll sit in there, or in warmer months at the herring run, and my thoughts will turn to things in my past that Mrs. Apps says are all water over the damned. She's been here for two years. In the last months that I've really gotten to know her, Mrs. Apps has said a lot of true things. My memories are a fact, however, and they say this: The order I've made in my life shapes up as so much bushwa.

For example, I remember a fourth-grade classroom in a big brick school set in a field of tar. Around the school there was a deep pit, like a moat separating the red brick from the tar, and along its length were two levels of black pipe. You could sit on the uppermost pipe and hook your feet behind the bottom one and look into the pit. The Haffenreffer brewery was across the street from the fourth-grade's plot in the yard. The sense of its bulk carried easily over the six-foot iron spiked fence at the outer edge of the tar. In fact, the sight and sour odor of the brewery dominated all the classrooms whose windows were on that side of the school. I had Miss McDowell for the fourth-grade. She was one of a handful of lay teachers. It was a break for most of us, sick of nuns, but her room was on the brewery side.

On the day I always remember there were two plainclothes policemen standing at the front of the class making the blackboard look very small. They wanted to know who had killed the sixth-grade brother of Francis Xavier Mooney. I shared a double desk with Francis Mooney. He was a slow boy with a gift for calligraphy who'd come over speaking only Gaelic. He never raised his eyes that day from his artwork on the desktop. When the two policemen moved on to the next room to ask the same unanswered question, Miss McDowell, who wasn't in the schoolyard when it happened, asked in sobs how any of us could have stood and watched two little boys stick one another with knives. I suppose, even now, I could only tell her that they didn't look little to me from where I was, with my insteps hooked behind the lower pipe, watching Mooney's sixth-grade brother dying in the pit. The other boy I knew only as Munk, and I don't think he went to school.

A carriage house sits across the road, a stone's throw from my window, unused and probably rotting. Or needing paint. I used to paint houses. I was a student then, and my wife-to-be taught piano to the daughters of municipal workers. We pooled

our money and married much later, when I'd finished my stud-
ies and begun to put them to work for me. In Azerbaijan they
say delayed sex leads to a longer life.

The carriage house was wedged among acres of woods once.
That land is privately developed now, was long before I got here,
and if I seem to be rambling it's not on account of my age, but
because my thoughts are cluttered with history. At college I had
a gifted teacher who claimed that historians only sweep up
after the actors. In any case I'm not talking about me, or about
this place, or even about Mrs. Apps, who looks a lot like Deborah Kerr did opposite Robert Mitchum in *The Sundowners*. She
reads to me nights.

She reads me popular novels and sometimes a play, and I tell
her the things that are most on my mind, stories like those
about Dennis Stuart and the two boys in the pit. I don't think
she's interested in my stories as stories, but that she senses
something in them about both of our lives. So at bedtime I wait
for her in my room. She comes when there's time. The books
she brings are all her own. When she's done she stacks each one
neatly on the mantel above a useless hearth, as if for the next
tenant. Fires of any sort here in the rooms are prohibited by
state law, though it's a big room and I pay enough for it to have
it to myself. Otherwise we couldn't talk as we've done these last
weeks. And she could never have read me through the fall, and
now this early winter month.

Her voice is chipper and pitiless. "Is anything all right?"
she'll say. Her hair is auburn. I think she looks right into my
eyes. I'm reminded of an old, old friend, a Postal official who
was asphyxiated on his way home from work when he charged
into a burning building that was, in fact, uninhabited. He'd
worked once under a man who drank to such an extent that he
developed a rhinal abscess so large it appeared he had two
ghastly noses. Unlike others, this friend took not only to looking directly at his superior's nose, but to speaking into it as well.

Mrs. Apps's husband is unemployed. He's a secondary school
teacher, and had worked here on the South Shore. He was let go
because of declining enrollment. After two years he's finally got

another job, so she'll be leaving here soon. He's going to work at his family's retail appliance store in Halifax, Nova Scotia. He's really trying to put his life in order, she says, and I wonder if she wouldn't rather see him dead. If she comes tonight I know the story I'll tell.

It concerns my cousin, killed in Havana in 1898. I was raised thinking of my cousin as a hero, and visited his pictures. On the walls of his father's house I saw him, uniformed, at Santiago Harbor, on liberty in Tampa, and grinning on the deck of the *Indiana*. In 1917, faced with the prospect of my own enlistment in that war, my mother confided to me about my cousin's death. She told me he returned drunk from liberty and stumbled from a gangplank. He was somehow crushed, and disappeared beneath the dock. A letter received by my aunt shortly afterward, signed by one of her son's comrades, had more or less attributed his bender to an argument with a local prostitute, who hadn't enough sense to see the wisdom of what amounts to my cousin's last request, that she follow him to Dorchester, Massachusetts.

The things I remember.

Down the hall a woman several years my junior is screaming, "Damn fool! Ya damn fool!" over and over.

"And are you a damn fool, Millie?" I can hear Mrs. Apps ask her.

"I am *not* a Democrat! Never been a Democrat!" the old lady yells.

Mrs. Apps is only thirty years old, younger than any of my children, who are all well educated, all well-to-do, and who seldom now bother to visit with me. My affairs are in the hands of my eldest son, a lawyer, my executor.

Last night Mrs. Apps told me about a conversation she overheard on a trolleycar in Boston this past weekend. It was between two teenage boys. I remember it pretty well. The first boy, mimicking his father, says:

" 'Don't you *ever* kick a man when he's down!' "

The second boy asks, "What's wrong with that?"

" 'Get him when he's about halfway up,' he told me."

"He said that?"

"The guy'd be completely off balance then—no way he's gonna block it."

"Muthah," says the second one.

"About the only good tip he ever gimme."

"What a muthah."

"A saint," says the first, "man's a saint."

The words of the boy who'd mimicked his dad caused me to remember something not really far from my mind, something my own father had impressed upon me. It was his claim that everything had a use, and if it came to that, a reason, and that the dead serve the living. But the boy on the trolleycar, even as a teenager, and Mrs. Apps, so young a woman, they both sense in their own instinctive way that that isn't true. My father was mistaken.

In the summer of 1929 my wife was washed off a rock at Martin's Beach, California, and drowned there in the surf. I was doing well, we'd never had a real honeymoon, and I had to fly to San Francisco for my employer so I took her along at my own expense. Late one afternoon we drove south, looking for a beach like we'd seen in a picture of the sun setting off Big Sur, and found one where because of the surf and the undertow there was no swimming. We hadn't intended to swim, we weren't dressed for it, and my wife had drunk half a bottle of white wine. We walked along the foot of a cliff until we came to a sandy cove. It was there that she saw her rock. It was carpeted with a silky green algae, and its flat surface extended out into the Pacific like a reviewing stand from the base at the far point of the cliff. Further out, the waves splattered against solitary, big black-looking rocks while the sun went down as red as either of us had ever seen it.

"It's prehistoric here, isn't it?" she said.

My wife was an athletic woman and she was wearing boat shoes, but I asked her to be careful of her footing on the wet algae. I rolled my trouser cuffs and followed in my bare feet, staying close to the cliff face. When she rounded the point she stopped suddenly, then moved casually away, to the sea. A wave that broke no higher than her ankles over the side of the rock swept her feet from under her and she was carried over the edge as if she were sliding on ice. Though I got out there on my hands and knees, my wife never surfaced. I had to cling to the edge of that rock like a crab until I was saved by a young man from Palo Alto. He said my wife had come around the point and seen him and his friend, a Stanford woman, lying on the rock with their limbs entangled. Both were in bathing suits. I know what my wife thought. But the woman had only slipped on the algae and the man, in trying to break her fall, had come down on top of her. When I imagine it now I can't help seeing the two as Burt Lancaster and Deborah Kerr in the love scene on the beach in *From Here to Eternity*.

Mrs. Apps says there's nothing wrong in that. She'll also tell you that she rents her white nursing shoes.

"I'm on my feet so much," she once said to me, "I have to keep buying those Dr. Scholl's air-cushioned innersoles, and then I wear right through them. At a dollar eighty-nine a pair for those things, I might as well be renting my shoes."

"Aren't we all," I said. "I was a square-jawed fella with a thick head of hair and a good smile once."

"Robert Mitchum," she said.

"I was taller, too. You shrink."

"Burt Lancaster!"

The market crash in October brought me out of my funk. I worked hard, remarried, had four healthy children, and again survived my wife. In the Second World War, I got a field-grade commission and then a presidential commendation for designing overseas military installations. I've done everything on earth that I was expected to do. I've outlived my responsibility to any person or thing in this life or any other, whether I like it or not.

Mrs. Apps has let me hear the desperate sound of her fingers as they smooth back the pages of each new book.

"Without knowing it you've helped to shatter the sense of orderliness of my life," I said to her recently. She took my hand so hard I swore.

"I've only opened the barn door after the horse has gone," she said.

I'd like to help her, too.

They're at the piano now, downstairs in the study, where the shelves are lined with volumes of Dickens, *Reader's Digest* Condensed Books, and an *Encyclopedia Britannica*. Mrs. Crawford, one of the older aides, is plodding through some bedtime show tune for a few of her regulars. The rhythm feints in and then out again under my door, a choppy, parlor treatment like that of how many little girls I don't remember. A little Rodgers and Hammerstein, a little of Dolly Wassiliew. Something from *The King and I*. Yesterday I overheard her talking to Mrs. Apps about her husband.

"I'm beginning to think like he does," she'd said. "He says he'll work until he dies, and that doesn't sound so bad to me as it did before I came to work here."

"Oh? What is it he does," asked Mrs. Apps, "that he'd like to die doing it?"

"He's got a *Boston Globe* distributorship," Mrs. Crawford told her. "He delivers *The Globe*. Not that he'll read it. He thinks *The Globe* wants to be mayor of Boston so it can ship all the minorities over to Harvard. That wouldn't be so bad, I said, but he said then we'd have them running our lives, too. But anyway he delivers it, all around here . . ."

I have a sister living. Brenda is seventy-six, and still clerks full-time in a dime store. Her husband is dead now, but she's recently become engaged to a retired milkman from South Boston. At Easter and on Christmas day her son Frank charitably drives her here. We sit in the study, and while we chat she says several rosaries on my behalf. Frank usually waits outside in the car, as hopeful I think as I am of a short visit.

I've of course lost my faith and a lot more, so Brenda's visits only recreate, in her kind gifts of long-remembered favorite foods and bits of small talk, many of the moods and smells from my youth. Now, for example, just thinking about her next visit I remember a young man who used to come here with my daughter. He was born and raised in my old neighborhood in Boston, and wrote a story once about another young man there named Corey. The store takes place long after I left the neighborhood, but when the manuscript was read to me I could see, blind even as age is making me, every shred of detail.

This young Corey was a thoughtful man who drank in good

company. One night while watching a card game in what the author describes as a raggy gin mill, he confronts, in a seemingly thoughtless act, a drunken animal of a man. The man has broken the bar window with his fist. He stands an instant with his back to the door, staring down the narrow passage between the single row of tables and the bar. Blood runs onto the floor from his cut knuckles. No one moves until Corey gets up from his table and steps in the man's path. No one speaks. Then the bartender leaps over the bar and shoves them both out the door. In the end Corey is standing outside under the Ladies Invited sign, literally dead on his feet, his throat cut with the jagged neck of a Budweiser bottle. There are a lot of eyewitnesses to what happens, but all anyone can say for sure about it is that he got up out of his chair when he could have remained in it. The drunken man's anger was intended for someone else, unaware in the men's room, where he was in the habit of passing out in the only stall. So why did Corey do it?

That story I'll save for next Monday night, Mrs. Apps's last night before leaving here for good. And on Monday night I'll tell her everything I've learned from these memories of a lifetime. Every secondhand thing I know about the virtue of an unnatural death.